PENGUIN CRIME FICTION

COUNTERSTROKE

"Having native originality, Andrew Garve imitates nobody, not even himself. There are other worthies writing today, but unlike them Garve does not work by formula and is not lured by the will o' the wisp of making the detective story a real novel: It has always been real, and Garve shows us what the genre ought now to be." —Jacques Barzun

"Mr. Garve is a mystery writer with a pleasant difference, or rather a number of differences. At a time when suspense is in surprisingly short supply in many of the works which bear that stamp, he provides a great deal of suspense." —*Wall Street Journal*

"Garve is as nimble with a plot as a skilled trout fisherman with his line." —*Dallas Times-Herald*

"Andrew Garve's predictability is rare—his books are uniformly excellent and always different." —*Washington Star*

BOOKS BY ANDREW GARVE

Andrew Garve

Counterstroke

PENGUIN BOOKS

Penguin Books Ltd, Harmondsworth,
Middlesex, England
Penguin Books, 625 Madison Avenue,
New York, New York 10022, U.S.A.
Penguin Books Australia Ltd, Ringwood,
Victoria, Australia
Penguin Books Canada Limited, 2801 John Street,
Markham, Ontario, Canada L3R 1B4
Penguin Books (N.Z.) Ltd, 182–190 Wairau Road,
Auckland 10, New Zealand

First published in the United States of America by
Thomas Y. Crowell, Publishers, 1978
Published in Penguin books by arrangement with
Thomas Y. Crowell, Publishers, 1979

Library of Congress Cataloging in Publication Data
Winterton, Paul, 1908–
    Counterstroke.
    Reprint of the ed. (c1978) published by Crowell,
New York.
    I. Title.
PZ3.W7354Co   1979   [PR6073.I56]   823'.9'12   79-15290
ISBN 0 14 00.5270 4

Printed in the United States of America by
Offset Paperback Mfrs., Inc., Dallas, Pennsylvania
Set in Granjon

PART ONE

THE PLAN

The night the news broke about Sally Morland I was feeling pretty sorry for myself. Not, I hasten to assure any reader, that self-pity is to be the keynote of this history. Far from it. I just happened that night to be in an acutely depressed mood, for two good and separate reasons—and if I hadn't been, there'd have been no story to tell.

I'd been dining with my agent, John Borley. John was the host—which was just as well, since we were eating at the legendary and expensive Giglio's, the in place over many years for theatrical big shots and their associates. Giglio—tall for an Italian, handsome, iron-haired—was courteous to me, deferential to John. He had—and who can blame him?—sensitive antennae for status, influence, and a credit card in good standing, none of which I could currently lay claim to. He ushered John, as a matter of course, to the alcove table, which in the unanimous view of the habitués was the most desirable in the restaurant. You could be noticed there but not easily stared at, and you had a commanding view of everyone else. In better days I'd been given the alcove quite often myself.

John was a plump, relaxed, and unmistakably prosperous man, somewhere short of sixty. He was rather more to me than the shrewd ten-percenter who had handled my bookings through several good years to our mutual profit; he was by way of being a friend and counselor as well.

As the martinis arrived, I said in a phony-casual tone, "Anything from Friedman yet?"

There was the briefest pause. Then John said, "Yes, Bob—he rang me this afternoon. Misery, I'm afraid . . . It seems he's changed his mind."

I said "Oh," and took a gulp of martini. It was a bitter blow. I'd been hoping, almost praying, that Friedman would come through with a firm offer. It would have meant resurrection for me. It would have meant a good role in thirteen episodes of a TV crime series—and I'd had the impression it was almost in the bag.

"Do you know who gets the part?" I asked.

John toyed with an olive. "Yes. Probably Felix Grant."

"Grant, eh?" Grudgingly I added, "He'll do it well."

"Not as well as you could have done, Bob. . . . Of course, he had certain advantages."

I thought I knew what John meant. Grant was known to have inherited a sizable fortune. He could afford to be seen in the top places with the top people. Money gave him the confidence, the independence, that impressed producers and directors. He didn't have to seek jobs—he could wait to be approached. So naturally he *was* approached. It was as simple as that. If you're known to be a struggling man, you're by-passed. If you don't need the job, you get it. Nothing succeeds like success. If I'd had a million dollars in the bank, I'd have been approached, too.

John said, "I'm terribly sorry about it, Bob. I did everything I could. I pulled out all the stops."

"I'm sure you did, John." I took another swig of martini, wishing it were hemlock. "It's such a bloody bore, though, doing nothing. I'm not cut out for inactivity. It's been months now, apart from the seaside shows. *Months*, John . . . And it isn't as though I was fussy. You know that. I'd do anything. I'd carry a spear at Stratford. I'd be the clock in the crocodile. Anything. I'm getting desperate."

"Something will come along," he said.

The Micawberish paraphrase didn't kid me. "I'm beginning to wonder. . . . There are hundreds of us jostling for jobs. Why should I be chosen? After all, I'm no more than a run-of-the-mill actor. Average talent, average looks, average bloody everything."

John shook his head. "That's not true. You're that very rare bird, an intelligent actor. You can talk sense without a script. . . . And in your own line, you're one of the finest in the business."

"In my own line? What does that amount to? Nobody can expect to make a living forever taking off top politicians."

"Look, Bob—eighteen months ago, Robert Farran was a household name. People talked and laughed about you on buses, in pubs, over the garden fence. 'Did you see Bob Farran last night—he was super.' And it'll happen again, I'm sure of it. In the end, it's personality that counts. Just now, the entertainment business is going through a bad patch—we all know it. Come to that, isn't everybody? But it won't last. You'll get another break before long. . . . The thing is, of course, to keep yourself in good shape for the opportunity when it comes. Know what I mean?"

"I'm not sure that I do."

John lit a cigarette. "Then I'd better give it to you straight," he said. "The word is that you're hitting the bottle pretty hard these days."

I looked at him uncomfortably. I couldn't deny it.

"Casting directors don't like that, you know."

I toyed with my empty glass. "Are you telling me the word reached Friedman?"

"I wouldn't be surprised, Bob."

So that was it. It was the booze, not the lack of a million dollars, that had cost me the job. Humiliating! Though I still thought that a million dollars might have helped.

"The days are empty," I said. "And the nights are lonely."

"I know, Bob. Believe me, I do understand. It was a hell of a thing to happen. The most appalling bad luck. Dreadful . . . But directors are hard men. They don't make allowances for private grief. All they're interested in is results. If they think someone is slipping, if they think the skids are under him, they look the other way. . . . You've got to snap out of it, my dear fellow. Take a grip on yourself. If not . . . Well, I don't need to dot the i's. You know the form as well as I do." He picked up the outsize menu. "Let's choose, shall we?"

2

It was after eleven when I got back to my scruffy Pimlico flat, high up under a Victorian slate roof. I glanced at the thermometer in the sitting room and it showed eighty-three degrees Fahrenheit. It had been like that all through the sweltering summer, and the first days of September had brought no relief. I stripped to my underpants and got some ice from the fridge. I filled up the glass with Scotch and swallowed a mouthful and sat glooming about the outturn of the evening.

John had meant well—and of course he was right. The way I was going, I was a man with a past and no future. A bum. I knew it. Every day I was sliding a little farther downhill. Drinking into my small capital at an alarming rate. Rapidly approaching destitution. Falling apart as a person . . . Oh, yes, John was right. But I needed more than advice—I needed something to do, something to take my mind off things, something to concentrate on. . . .

Maybe if I went along to the labor exchange they'd find me some unskilled job to keep body and soul in proximity—though these days, with a million and a half unemployed and everyone cutting down, you couldn't even count on getting taken on as a road sweeper. Anyway, I didn't want to be a road sweeper. Even less did I want public relief for doing nothing. I wanted, desperately, to do the job I'd been trained for. In any capacity.

I looked blearily across at Mary's picture. Time would heal everything, friends had said. Maybe they were right—but how much time? Half a year hadn't helped. The hurt was as sharp, the memory as poignant as ever. We had been so happy—so positively, exuberantly happy—and then suddenly the dark. . . . Perhaps, I thought, I should put her picture away in a drawer. It did nothing for me now, except to bring maudlin tears to my eyes when I was full of drink. Soon, with its sculpted look and static smile, it wouldn't even do that. 'Forever wilt thou love and she be fair.' What a lot of cock!

I downed the rest of the whisky. I wasn't drunk, but I was muzzy. Well on the way now to a few hours of blessed oblivion. My watch, if I read the hands aright, showed just on midnight. I switched on the radio, more from habit than interest, and caught the tail end of a news item that the announcer said had just come in. Some woman had been found shot dead in remotest Suffolk, and fears were being entertained for the safety of Mrs. Sally Morland. The name meant nothing to me, but the idea of fears being entertained set me off giggling. In the state I was in, it seemed as funny as a final income-tax demand I'd once had—"steps would be put in hand." Hilarious! After I'd stopped giggling, I switched off the radio and groped my way to my unmade bed.

3

I woke late, with the thin edge of a well-deserved headache. Sunshine was streaming into the flat, and the bedroom was oven-hot in spite of open windows. I took another look at the thermometer. Eighty Fahrenheit—and still not a hint of any storm to break the endless drought. The English weather pattern seemed to have gone haywire. I made some coffee, swallowed a couple of aspirins, slipped on a light dressing gown over nothing, and went downstairs to collect my newspaper from the communal hall table. There were several others there besides my *Record*, and they all carried huge headlines, which for once were not about the economic crisis. The *Record*'s were:

FRANK MORLAND'S WIFE KIDNAPPED

NEIGHBOUR SHOT DEAD

KIDNAPPERS' DEMAND—"RELEASE TOM LACEY"

TORTURE THREAT

Frank Morland! Now the name *did* ring a bell—and the large type was explained. Back in the flat, I drank my coffee and read the story. The account ran:

Mrs. Sally Morland, wife of Mr. Frank Morland, M.P., the Minister for Export Promotion, was kidnapped yesterday evening from their country home, Broom Cottage, near Levenham, East Suffolk. A neighbour, Mrs. Elaine Jeffries, who lived alone in a house immediately opposite, was found shot dead beside Mrs. Morland's Rover car in the cottage drive.

A man claiming to be one of the kidnappers telephoned the *Post* shortly after midnight with the message "We are holding Sally Morland. We will exchange her for Tom Lacey. We shall communicate with the authorities in nine days' time to learn their decision. Unless they agree to the exchange, Mrs. Morland will be tortured to death."

Tom Lacey, a self-confessed anarchist, was sentenced to life imprisonment a year ago for the murder of a security guard during a North London pay-roll snatch by a gang which got away with £75,000. The rest of the gang escaped by car and have never been traced. It is assumed that these men were responsible for yesterday's outrage.

Parcels found in the Rover car suggest that the two women had been out shopping together. It is thought that they had just turned in to the cottage drive and were getting out of the car when the kidnappers attacked, riddling Mrs. Jeffries with sub-machine-gun bullets, and carrying off Mrs. Morland. The alarm was raised at 11 P.M. by a passing motorist, Mr. Fred Angel of Bury St. Edmunds, who stopped to investigate after his car lights had picked out the body lying in the drive.

The Morlands have been married for three years. Mrs. Morland, 25, is the daughter of Dr. Patrick McQueen, formerly of Belfast, and now in practice in Exeter. She is an active political worker and a very popular figure in her husband's constituency. Mr. Morland, 39, who won the East Suffolk division at the last General Election by the narrow majority of 220, is regarded as one of his Party's "bright hopes" and a probable future Cabinet Minister. He was appointed Minister for Export Promotion in the reshuffle last April. Before joining the administration he was active in the City and controlled a group of property and finance companies. He is reputed to be a multimillionaire.

That was the end of the text, but there were also several photographs. One was of Sally Morland, an attractive brunette. One was of Morland, handsome and alert and looking every inch the rising politician. One was of Tom Lacey, a youngish man with a full beard and mustache, eyes of some light color, and a face of no special distinction.

4

As I showered and shaved, I mulled somberly over the happening. A few years back—a mere ten years, perhaps—such an item of news would have seemed hardly credible. Times had certainly changed. Now kidnappings with violence had become almost a commonplace in the world, the routines standardized and familiar. An innocent victim seized, a chance witness quickly disposed of, a telephone call to a newspaper, the terms laid down, the time limit set, the threat spelled out. It was a growth industry, one of the few. Such snatches happened so often that one's sense of horror became blunted. It was like reading about casualties in a long and bloody war. . . . But, so far, kidnappings had occurred only rarely in comparatively peaceful England—and even more rarely of someone in the public eye, in a quiet English country lane. This was an outrage on one's own doorstep. So the drama could still grip, the stark headlines still shock.

What stayed in the mind was that gruesome sentence,

". . . Mrs. Morland will be tortured to death." Not just got rid of, not just killed—the suffering would go on and on. It was a calculated frightener, of course—putting the maximum pressure on the authorities. Unless the kidnappers were sadists, it was hard to believe they would actually go that far. If their demand was turned down, what would be the point? Yet could one be sure? If you make threats and don't carry them out, you lose credibility for the next time. If you do carry them out, you've gained ground for the next time. No future decision-maker would be likely to forget how a helpless girl had been slowly and agonizingly destroyed.

I thought of Morland. He must be living through a private hell. "Tortured to death." Christ, what a thing to hear about someone you loved. To imagine! Suppose it had been Mary . . . I'd have been out of my mind. Begging on my knees. Begging for surrender . . .

5

On my way out to lunch I bought a midday *Star*. Its reporters had been able during the morning to fill in some of the gaps in the brief overnight account, and its front and center pages were entirely given over to the story.

It was now established, I read, that Mrs. Morland had driven Mrs. Jeffries into the local market town of Blatchford in the early afternoon of the previous day. Mrs. Jeffries was elderly and too arthritic to drive a car of her own, and it had been Sally Morland's kindly custom to take her into the town at least once a week. On this occasion, they had done their usual shopping and had then gone to a cinema. This information came from the box-office girl and from a municipal car-park attendant, both of whom knew Mrs. Morland by sight and both of whom had exchanged a few words with her. Assuming the two ladies had seen the program through, they would have left Blatchford for Broom Cottage at about 8:30 P.M. Apparently someone in the Levenham neighborhood had heard what sounded like distant shots just before 9 P.M.— which fitted in with the rest of the evidence. It had, of course, been quite dark by then, which helped to account for the kidnappers' easy getaway.

There was an explanatory paragraph about the Morlands' domestic arrangements, which had played their part in the tragedy. It seemed that Sally and Frank Morland had kept up two homes: Broom Cottage in the constituency, practically a must for an M.P.; and a flat in Belgravia, which was mainly used as a *pied-à-terre* by Morland when he was detained by late sittings and departmental duties. He had been at the London flat when, in the early hours of the morning, the police had called with news of the kidnapping. Mrs. Morland, because she disliked being alone during the week in a rather isolated cottage, had had for some time a Swedish *au pair* girl living with her— a Miss Helma Lindquist, from Malmö, who was perfecting her English. Miss Lindquist—fortunately or unfortunately—had been invited to stay with friends in London on the night of the kidnapping. It was not unlikely that the kidnappers had been aware of her absence.

There were various other snippets of news and views. There was mention of a lay-by close to Broom Cottage— a Council dump for road chippings—which the kidnappers might have used as an observation post, noting departures and returns. There was mention of a bend in the lane opposite the cottage, which was why Fred Angel, the passing motorist, had been able to pick out the body in his headlights. There were a few facts about the police investigation on the spot. The cottage drive had been thoroughly examined, but no useful clues had been found. The Rover car was being checked for fingerprints as a routine measure, though it was assumed the raiders would have worn gloves. The man who had telephoned the *Post* had had "an educated accent," which, rare though it might be in an age of do-it-yourself schooling, was hardly an identifying trait. In short, little progress had been made. The kidnappers had got clean away, and no one had the slightest idea who they were or where Mrs. Morland was being held.

On the latter point, the *Star*'s chief crime reporter somewhat narrowed the field. "There is no reason to doubt," he wrote, "that the kidnappers and their victim are still in this country. Although, as probable adherents of what is sometimes called 'the radical underground,' the gang might have hoped for sanctuary in some country unfriendly to Britain while they attempted to negotiate their proposed exchange, the fact is that they would have had little chance of getting away. Departure through any of the normal exit channels, with a captive woman, would obviously have been so difficult as to be almost impossible. Theoretically they could have left last night in some unorthodox way, such as by light plane, but they would have been certain to run into refuelling problems before reaching safe territory. An additional pointer is that the man who telephoned the *Post* after midnight spoke from a British call-box. The night switchboard operator at the *Post* is certain that the pips were of the usual domestic type.

13

Assuming, as the police do, that the kidnappers are still in this country, they have now no choice but to keep their victim here, as all ports, airfields and coastguard stations have been alerted and are on round-the-clock watch."

The report added: "An unusual feature of the kidnapping is the nine-day gap before a decision on the exchange is required. Most kidnappers are eager to get rid of their hostage at the earliest possible moment, since the difficulties of keeping anyone hidden become increasingly formidable as the days go by. Mrs. Morland's kidnappers appear to be extremely confident about the security of their hideout."

The *Star*'s political correspondent had a reflective piece about possible moves by the Government. He wrote:

An emergency Cabinet meeting was being called this morning to consider the Morland kidnapping. It is understood that Mr. Frank Morland was likely to be present. While nothing is yet known of the Government's intentions, it is clear that Ministers are caught in a hideous dilemma. It is only two weeks ago that the Prime Minister spoke out in the strongest terms against what he called "the short-sighted cowardice" of some (unnamed) countries in surrendering to terrorist threats. "I would like to make it absolutely plain," he said, "that whatever the circumstances of the case, this Government will never feed the crocodile." In the light of that unequivocal commitment it seems inconceivable that the Government could now hand over Tom Lacey in exchange for Mrs. Morland. However, in the past many governments have weakened in the face of intolerable circumstances and unthinkable horrors. The Cabinet's choice in the Morland case is particularly cruel since Frank Morland is a well-liked colleague and Mrs. Morland is personally known with affection both in her husband's constituency and among Cabinet Ministers and their wives. Will this, therefore, be regarded as a special case? The police would certainly be opposed to any surrender. Though fully realising what could be at stake, they argue that Tom Lacey is an outstandingly dangerous anarchist, a proved and callous killer who, once released, would be most likely to kill again in association with his gang. One life, one person's agony, must therefore be weighed against the possible fate of others. It would appear that several members of the Cabinet strongly hold the view that exchanging Tom Lacey for Mrs. Morland would also boost the morale of other criminal groups and encourage them to adopt similar methods. In short, there would be no net reduction in human suffering.

It seemed to me a good piece, putting the issues squarely. I felt thankful that *I* didn't have to make the decision.

6

By now, like millions of others, I was hooked on the case, and I tuned in to most of the news bulletins throughout the day. There were one or two fresh items, but they were quite peripheral. Sally Morland's father, Dr. McQueen, had traveled up from Exeter and was seeing Morland, and possibly some Cabinet Ministers. Miss Lindquist, the Swedish *au pair,* had given a tearful interview to the press, which had added nothing except emotion. One or two sinister goings-on had been investigated. Police had followed up a story from Huddersfield that a woman had been carried into a house by two men at night, but it had turned out that the woman was a cripple and the men had been her sons. Until six o'clock, no development of any significance was reported. Then there came a dramatic announcement.

Frank Morland, through his solicitors, had offered the kidnappers £250,000 in cash for the safe return of his wife, and was prepared to start negotiations at once for the hand-over. The B.B.C.'s political correspondent commented: "It seems likely that the Cabinet have given their reluctant approval to this approach. As a private offer, it doesn't commit the Government in any way, and if accepted it would certainly be a welcome alternative to the surrender of Tom Lacey. At the same time it can be taken as an indication that the Government has no present intention of giving way on the main issue."

As an armchair observer of the drama, I had a few private thoughts about Morland's offer and its likely reception. It seemed to me that a gang which had so easily acquired £75,000 in a payroll snatch only a year ago, and could doubtless acquire more lolly by similar means at any time, would hardly be tempted by Morland's financial bait, with all the dangers attendant on the picking up of ransom money. And, as it turned out, I was right.

The final word that day came in a late B.B.C. broadcast. In a curt message, phoned to the *Post* news desk by the man with the educated voice, the answer had been: "We are not interested in two hundred and fifty thousand pounds. We are interested only in the release of Lacey."

7

It was an oppressively hot night again, far too hot for easy sleep. I lay naked on the bed with a corner of sheet over my vitals, and because I had little else to think about

I went on thinking about the kidnapping. About the callous brutality of it all. About Mrs. Jeffries, an old arthritic woman gunned down because she happened to be in the way. About Sally Morland, alone and helpless in the hands of unknown thugs in an unknown place, with no chance of rescue. (Though it did cross my mind—would I have been giving her plight so much thought if she'd been an ugly old man and not an attractive young girl? Sex rearing its head?) Finally about Morland's rejected offer, the deadlock that had been reached, the mounting predicament of the decision-makers. They must be on the rack, those twenty or so members of the Cabinet. Humiliating surrender, or cruel abandonment—what a choice! And no third way open to them. No possibility of compromise. No hope of successful bluff or subterfuge . . .

Subterfuge!

It was at that moment that I was suddenly visited by one of those notions that startle by their vividness. Suddenly I was gripped by an idea. It was one of those ideas that seem absolutely brilliant in the half-conscious middle of the night, and absolutely crazy in the morning.

But the thing about this one was that it didn't seem *absolutely* crazy in the morning. It just seemed fairly crazy. A fanciful notion, certainly. Probably quite unrealistic. Probably impracticable. But it was something to toy with—something that might bear looking into further. After all, what else had I to do? When a day stretches blankly ahead, almost any occupation is better than none.

Thus it came about that, around ten o'clock, I phoned Leo Curtis, the *Record*'s theatre critic, at his home. I'd known Leo, not intimately but very agreeably, for several years. He had once written some very complimentary things about me in a review, which had started up a mutu-

17

ally valued on-and-off drinking companionship.

He was surprised by my early call, but not at all put out. We exchanged the usual civilities. Then I said, "Leo, does your paper have a cuttings library, by any chance?"

"Sure," he said. "All papers do. Why? What's on your mind?"

"I'm interested in the background of the Morland kidnapping. I'd like to try my hand at a script when it's all over, preferably before everyone else does, and that means getting cracking now on a bit of research. Studying the *dramatis personae* in depth. Morland and his wife. Boning up on anarchism. Checking back on the Lacey trial. That sort of thing . . . Do you suppose your people would let me see what they've got?"

"I should think so," Leo said. "I'll put in a word, shall I? When would you like to go along?"

"This morning?"

He chuckled. "A keen type, eh? Okay, Bob, I'll ring you."

He was back on the phone in half an hour. "Anytime after eleven-thirty," he said. "I shan't be in the office, but the librarian, Bill Chalmers, is expecting you. Just follow the red carpet! He's a fan of yours."

I thanked him warmly. I didn't have a wife, and I didn't have a job, but it seemed I still had friends.

8

I got to the *Record* office just before twelve. The doorman was expecting me, and a messenger boy conducted me through a maze of corridors to the library. Chalmers greeted me with a friendly handshake and some enthusiastic words about a program he'd seen me in in the distant past. He then found me a seat in one of the less busy corners, and produced the cuttings I was interested in—the file on Tom Lacey, and the file on the Morlands—together with Volume 1 of the Encyclopaedia Britannica.

I checked first on the facts of the payroll snatch that had ended Lacey's freedom. It had happened at an engineering plant on a new industrial estate at Willesden, on a Friday morning in the May of the previous year. A security van with two guards had driven up to the main entrance with the wages money. A car had followed them in. As the guards descended, there was a hail of shots, and both of them were mowed down beside the van. The noise brought a doorman and several workers out of the factory. The raiding car was already moving off with the loot, but one of the raiders was not yet in it. The rear door was open and he was running, poised to leap in. He was carrying a submachine gun, which suddenly seemed to get caught in his legs, and he stumbled and fell heavily. The car slowed for a moment, then roared away as the door was slammed from the inside. The factory men pounced on the dazed raider—who was Lacey. The whole incident had lasted hardly more than seconds, but £75,000 had gone, and there were two men dead. One of them, it was later established, had been killed by shots from Lacey's submachine gun. The raiding car was described by one of the factory men as gray, by another as blue. It had been seen only from the rear, and no one was sure of the make. No one had managed to get its number. One witness thought there had been two men in it as it sped away, one thought three. Anyhow, by the time the police arrived on the scene, it had disappeared into the heavy London traffic. A stolen car, which could have been the one used, was later found abandoned half a mile away, but it offered no clues to the raiders.

A great deal had subsequently been written about Lacey—though most of it was of a negative kind. He had given his name as Tom Lacey, but no one knew whether that was his real name. He had refused to give any other personal information. He had refused to say anything about the other members of the gang. His fingerprints were found to have no counterpart in criminal records, so there was no back history to help the inquiry. His photograph had been widely publicized on TV and in the press, with a police request that anyone who recognized him should come forward. Nearly a hundred people had responded, but no firm identification had been made. At the time of his capture he had had no papers or documents of any kind on his person: no wallet, no watch, no jewelry. He had been wearing an off-the-peg two-piece suit of a type sold in thousands by Marks & Spencer; cheap canvas shoes; rubber gloves that could have been bought from any drugstore; and the customary stocking mask. All identification marks on his gun had been obliterated. So he had remained Tom Lacey, a man without any known background, a man who had clearly taken the most stringent precautions to cover his tracks in case of trouble. As, presumably, the other members of the gang had done. There was planning here of unusual quality.

The trial had been brief. Asked how he wished to plead, Lacey had refused to recognize the court and had shouted "Long live anarchism!"—adding, so the record went, "The passion for destruction is also a creative passion." These unlikely words had subsequently been traced by literate newsmen to the nineteenth-century anarchist Mikhail Bakunin. A formal plea of not guilty had been entered on Lacey's behalf, but it had done him no good since he had been caught almost literally red-handed. After a verdict of guilty, and a few incisive remarks from the judge, he had been sentenced to imprisonment for life.

In several of the cuttings there were reporters' descriptions of Lacey as he had stood in the dock. "In his late twenties," someone had guessed—since he had consistently declined to give his age. "A well-built man of medium height." "Luxuriant russet beard, whiskers and moustache." "Crisp curling hair of the same colour, worn fairly short." "Unwavering stare from grey-blue eyes." "Quiet behaviour after initial outburst." "Coldly disdainful of the proceedings."

I turned to the cuttings on the Morlands—a bulging envelope of fact and gossip. First, Frank Morland. It seemed that he had been something of a City whiz-kid, a man well on the way to building a financial empire before he had abandoned it all for politics. The recorded details of interlocking companies and wide-ranging interests were too complex for me to follow, but the *Financial Times* had clearly found them absorbing. However, that part of his career was now all in the past. Morland had moved on— and the cuttings had moved on with him. As an M.P., and particularly as a Minister, he had been rated even more newsworthy. "Undoubtedly destined for high office" was the general view. "Perhaps a future Premier." A string of adjectives, most of them complimentary, built up the picture. "Handsome," "debonair," "ambitious," "well-informed," "witty," "self-confident," "astringent." In short, an unusually dynamic and positive personality. And, not

21

surprisingly, attractive to women. There were some gossip paragraphs, and a couple of photographs, linking him with various nubile girls before his marriage.

I concentrated next on Sally Morland. Among the cuttings there was a recent "profile" of her, contributed by some anonymous friend, which made it clear that she was not just the devoted wife of a rich and rising politician, but a considerable person in her own right. She had, it appeared, graduated at Cambridge, where she had specialized in botany. She had gone on from there to do postgraduate work in an esoteric branch of science called taxonomy (a new word to me), which I gathered from the writer was something to do with classification—in Sally's case, presumably of plants. She had involved herself in some intrepid traveling in the less comfortable parts of the Middle East, in the course of which she had stoically swallowed sheep's eyes and had narrowly evaded the attentions of a randy sheik. However, though essentially serious-minded and cerebrally dedicated to her work, she was apparently no bluestocking. That, at least, was her friend's view. She had, according to the writer, an exceptional gift for getting along with people. She had a gay and cheerful disposition, a pleasing voice with just a touch of the Irish in her speech, a delightful dimpled smile, and a healthily balanced outlook on life. If only half of this was true, the luckless Sally was obviously something of a paragon. If rather less was true, she was still evidently quite a girl.

She had met Frank Morland in Zermatt, where by chance they were staying at the same hotel. Morland was on a climbing holiday with a companion, preparing to make his second attempt on the Matterhorn without benefit of fixed ropes. Sally was doing field work with a study group. The two had fallen for each other at their first meeting, and after a "whirlwind romance"—so the cutting had it—they had married in London three months later, stylishly and with much publicity. Morland had been at that time a prospective Parliamentary candidate in the East Suffolk division, and Sally, though not a political animal, had thrown herself with characteristic zest into the election campaign that had shortly followed. The impact of her charm upon the voters had been considerable, and Morland had been the first to agree that with the narrow vote she had probably turned the balance in his favor. Latterly, she had been less active in the constituency, devoting much of her time at Broom Cottage to the writing of a thesis on some recondite matter connected with Turkish chickweed.

The file contained several pictures of Sally Morland, all of them better than the one I'd seen in the *Record*. She was undoubtedly attractive. Not exactly beautiful—but her face had the kind of delicate appeal that lingers in the mind. I could well understand Morland taking a header for her.

Finally, I opened the Encyclopaedia and turned up the article on anarchism. To my simple mind, anarchy equated with confusion and chaos, but I assumed there must be more to it than that. I read about a man called Godwin— William Godwin. A work called *Enquiry Concerning Political Justice*. Vaguely, from my student days, I remembered his name. He'd had something to do with Shelley. . . . I read about Proudhon. A visionary. Wanted an alternative society based on cooperation rather than coercion. What a hope! I read about Bakunin. A Russian nobleman turned conspirator. A barricades man. A street fighter. Violent

23

revolution the necessary prelude to heaven on earth. "We recognize no other activity but the work of extermination." Delightful fellow! I read about Malatesta, an Italian. "The insurrectionary deed is the most efficacious means of propaganda." I read through a list of notable anarchist assassinations. King Umberto I of Italy; the Empress Elizabeth of Austria; President Carnot of France; President McKinley . . . I read, "Some anarchist thinkers have refused to recognise any limitation on the individual's right to do as he will, or any obligation to act socially." Do your own thing, in fact. Very modern! I read, "Existing society is so corrupt that it has to be completely swept away." Total violence, as the way to total reconciliation. It made no sense to me. There was nothing constructive here. There was no indication of a practical alternative, of how the new society would work. These people were destroyers. Starting as woolly idealists and ending as butchers . . . Not, on the whole, a cheerful read. But interesting.

I thanked Chalmers for his help, and withdrew to a nearby pub to think over what I'd learned about the gang and Sally and Morland and Lacey—particularly Lacey—and to consider my idea again in the light of the facts I'd gleaned. I could see there would be immense difficulties. I didn't relish the thought of being treated as a complete ass for making the suggestion. I could well imagine the acid comments. Or worse—the hurried call for men in white coats! All the same, nothing I'd discovered so far ruled out the venture as impossible in my own mind. Indeed, in several respects I felt the outlook had improved. . . . I sat in my corner for nearly an hour, mulling things over and trying to decide what to do. Wondering how I should begin, if I did begin. Go to the police, I supposed, to Scotland Yard—since I had no access to the political corridors of power. After that, it would be up to them. I debated, hesitated, dithered. In the end I decided I might as well give it a try. Dip a toe in the water and see what it felt like. After all, I still had nothing else to do.

9

I had visited Scotland Yard only once before, as a small boy, when it was still modestly housed on the Victoria Embankment. I'd been taken there by my father, though I can't now recall what the occasion was. The imposing new place overlooking St. James's Park was unfamiliar. The great glass-and-concrete block, twenty stories high or thereabouts, looked as if it could cope with all the villains in the world—though, considering the way the crime rate was rising, I thought they'd probably have to build on pretty soon!

I pushed through one of the doors and looked around the reception area. To the right there was a kind of foyer with comfortable soft seats, like the anteroom of a plush West End cinema. Ahead there was a long counter, personed by two very presentable young policewomen disguised as civilians. To the left of the counter there was a guarded gate, the only visible approach to the upper regions. Tough-looking men waving passes were going through the gate in both directions in a fairly steady stream.

I approached the counter and said, rather diffidently, that I wished to see the Commissioner. Many actors, away from the footlights, tend to be diffident, and I was one of them. The girl gave me a form to fill in. I wrote my name, address, and profession, and "The Commissioner" in the appropriate place; and where they wanted to know the purpose of my visit I wrote, "Too important to put on paper." The girl ran a cool eye over my entry, and invited me to take a seat, which I did.

Ten minutes passed. Then a broad-shouldered man in a light gray suit came through the gate, spoke to one of the persons, and was directed toward me. He had my piece of paper in his hand. "Mr. Farran?" he asked.

"Yes," I said, getting up.

"I'm Sergeant Norris. What's it about, sir?"

"I wanted to see the Commissioner."

"Yes, sir . . ." Norris spoke in the patient tone of a man whose whole life was spent as a first line of defense against nut cases. "Unfortunately the Commissioner is not available at the moment. Now, if you could tell me what it's about . . ."

I said, "I'm reluctant to do that. It's a—a very secret matter."

A faint sound escaped him—the suspicion of a sigh. "If you won't tell me what it's about, sir, I'm afraid I shan't be able to help you."

"Well . . ." I hesitated. "It's to do with the Morland kidnapping."

"Oh? Have you information?"

"Not exactly information. But I have certain—knowledge. . . . I thought I might possibly be of some use."

"I see." The sergeant scrutinized me. "Well, would you just wait here, sir?"

I settled back in my comfortable chair, and watched the passing show. Ten, fifteen minutes went by. No developments. I began to wish I hadn't come. The small amount of confidence I'd had in my idea was steadily draining away. Maybe I should sneak out and forget the whole thing. . . . Then the sergeant reappeared. "Would you come this way, sir?"

I went with him through the gate, into a busy lift, along about a mile of corridor, and through a door. "Mr. Farran," Norris announced, and withdrew.

It was a small room, modestly furnished. There were two men in it. One was seated behind a desk on a swivel chair, the other on a chair at the side. The one behind the desk got up. He was a shortish, thickset man. He didn't look like a policeman; he looked like some small child's benign grandfather. "Please sit down, Mr. Farran," he said in a friendly tone, indicating another comfortable chair.

We all sat down.

"My name is Davey," he said. "I understand you have some information about the Morland case."

"Well—not exactly information," I said, "But—in certain circumstances—it's possible I might be able to help."

"In what way?"

"I would prefer to talk directly to the Commissioner. There's a security angle."

Davey looked down at my piece of paper. "Robert Farran. Actor." Somehow I felt I would have carried more weight if I'd written "Burglar." "Should I know your name, Mr. Farran?"

Rather snide, that, I thought, for a benign granddad. "I rather doubt it," I said.

He looked at the other man. "Do you know it, Sergeant?" He added apologetically, "This is Sergeant Fairlie." The sergeant and I nodded to each other.

Fairlie said, "Yes, sir, I do remember Mr. Farran. He used to be on television quite a bit. Taking off politicians. Did it very well, if I may say so."

Davey grunted, "I don't get much time for the box.

. . ." He swiveled back to me. "Anyhow, Mr. Farran, the position is this. Either you talk to me or you don't talk to anyone. It's up to you."

I got up from my chair. "In that case, I suppose I'd better go. It was just a thought. . . ." I moved toward the door.

A voice said, "You might just as well let me see him, Davey. What have we got to lose?"

Davey almost jumped out of his seat. His glance shot to the door, which was firmly closed. He glowered at me. "Do you *know* the Commissioner?"

"No," I said.

"Then how the devil—?"

"He was the guest speaker at an Equity dinner a week or two back. I'm sorry—it was a silly parlor trick. . . . I apologize for wasting police time."

Davey said, "Sit down, Mr. Farran." His tone left no room for argument, so I sat down. He was silent for a moment. Then he said, "I'm going to treat you as a sensible man, though so far I've no reason to do so. You want to see the Commissioner. Now, suppose I went along to him and said, 'Sir, I've a man in my room, an actor, who has something on his mind about the Morland case, but he won't tell me what it is, so will you see him?' How do you think he'd react? I'd get a rocket—and I'd damn well deserve it."

I nodded slowly. "Yes—I do understand. . . . But, as I said, there's a security angle. It really is a most secret and sensitive matter."

"Look, Mr. Farran, I happen to be a Deputy Assistant Commissioner. I'm in overall charge of the Morland case. I have more secrets under my belt than you've had hot dinners. I assure you that whatever you have to say will be safe with me. Now, then—what about it?"

I wavered. Perhaps I was being unreasonable. A Deputy Assistant Commissioner would hardly go around chattering about a case. "Well . . ." I paused. "Could we talk alone?"

Davey motioned to the sergeant. "Wait outside, Ben, will you? Not too far away!" Some significant glance briefly linked the two men. As Fairlie passed me, he said, "Excuse me, sir," and deft hands moved quickly around me. "Clean," he announced, and departed.

Davey said, "Sorry about that, Mr. Farran, but we do have to be a bit careful. There are so many screwballs around these days. . . . Now, let's hear what's on your mind."

10

I still found it difficult to tell him, without some sort of defensive preamble. Especially after his remark about screwballs.

"I *would* like to stress," I said, "that it's no more than a suggestion. I realize it might not come to anything. And of course if the Cabinet decided to let Tom Lacey go in exchange for Mrs. Morland, it wouldn't even arise. But they're obviously in a terrible dilemma and this could be the one way of getting them off the hook, and—"

Davey cut me short. "What *is* your suggestion, Mr. Farran?"

"My suggestion is that I should impersonate Tom Lacey, and be exchanged for Mrs. Morland."

If he was surprised—and he must have been—he didn't show it. He just gazed at me wonderingly.

"And why would you want to do that?" he asked.

"For the money," I said.

"What money?"

"Mr. Morland offered the kidnappers two hundred and fifty thousand pounds for the safe return of his wife, and they turned him down. If I could bring about her safe return by impersonating Lacey, I should expect the same amount from him."

"Just a quarter of a million pounds, eh?" Davey's tone was sardonic.

"Well, I suppose the figure might be negotiable. . . . It does sound rather a lot of money, I know, but Morland's a rich man and he did make the offer, so you must admit it's a perfectly logical sum to ask."

"Oh, it's logical, all right. . . . So your reasons are mercenary."

"Broadly speaking, yes. Though naturally, like everyone else, I'd be delighted to see Mrs. Morland safe and free."

"Have you any idea what Tom Lacey looks like?"

"I've a rough idea. At least, I've an idea what he looked like when he was convicted. I've read descriptions of him. I've seen some newspaper photographs. . . . Mind you, I'm not saying it could be done. That would depend on many things. It's—well, something I thought could be explored. No more than that."

"Would you say he looks anything like you?"

"We seem to have one or two basic things in common. Medium build, medium height. Blue-gray eyes, so one of the papers said . . . What really matters is that he doesn't look *unlike* me, in any striking way. He hasn't got a Cyrano nose or a long chin or a humped back—and neither have I. He's kind of average. An ordinary sort of appearance— like mine. You can do a lot with an ordinary appearance—

it makes a good working surface. . . . Of course, I'd need to know much more about him before I could judge whether a convincing impersonation was possible."

Davey slowly shook his head. "It's an intriguing notion, Mr. Farran—but I just can't see it happening. I don't believe you could ever get away with it."

"You may be right—but I'd say it's early days to take a view. You'd be amazed what a little practice and a bit of make-up can do."

"H'm . . . You do realize, don't you, that this gang are just about as ruthless as any we've ever had to deal with. They shot two men dead in the payroll robbery. They gunned down Mrs. Jeffries without a qualm. They're now threatening to torture Mrs. Morland to death if their terms aren't met—and it's quite possible they'll do so. . . . What do you suppose would happen to you if they found out— as I'm sure they would—that you were not Tom Lacey, but an impostor? Have you no imagination?"

"It's because I have imagination," I said, "that I'm asking for a lot of money. Obviously there would be a risk. I just have a feeling—a professional feeling—that I might be able to pull it off. Though, as I say, I'd need to know a lot more. . . ."

"You did mention that," Davey said dryly. "Tell me— have you had any experience of cloak-and-dagger work?"

"None at all."

"Have you ever used a gun?"

"Only on the stage."

"Could you hope to defend yourself against an armed thug?"

"Not physically, no. I'm not setting up as a James Bond. I'd have to rely on my wits."

"Which can be scattered by a single bullet. Oh, well

. . ." Davey drew a pad toward him. "Let's have some particulars about you. Is Robert Farran your full name?"

"No . . . Robert Linsley Farran."

"Where were you born?"

"Blackheath."

"How old are you?"

"Thirty-one."

"Are you married?"

"Not now . . ."

The pencil hovered. "Divorced?"

"No. My wife died."

"Ah . . . Some accident, was it?"

"No—leukemia."

"When did that happen, Mr. Farran?"

"Seven months and eight days ago."

"I see." There was a slight pause. "Any children?"

"No."

"Parents alive?"

"No."

"What happened to them?"

"My father was a fireman. He fell off a scorching ladder trying to get a kid out of a window. He was a very tenacious man—but you can't hold on when you're burning. They gave him a medal. Posthumously, of course. My mother died soon afterwards."

"H'm . . . A sad family history."

"Yes."

"Have you any close relatives?"

"I've a married sister in Adelaide—but you can't be close at that range. There are one or two aunts and uncles who might come to my funeral if they heard about it—but I rarely see them."

"Are you living alone?"

"Yes."

"Any—attachments?"

"No."

"Are you working?"

"No—I'm unemployed."

"What are you living on?"

"The fag end of my savings . . . There's no dole for free-lance actors, you know."

"I didn't know that. . . . Well, now, I've got your address here. Have you a telephone number?"

I gave it to him.

He sat quietly for a moment, doodling on his pad, frowning in thought. He was a man, I guessed, who'd been carried a little out of his depth by unfamiliar currents. The Morland affair, with its political overtones, was no ordinary crime. Finally he said, "Do you mind waiting here, Mr. Farran?" He went to the door and called Sergeant Fairlie in. They exchanged a few words, *sotto voce*, and Davey departed.

11

The sergeant was amiable. He was, as he'd already indicated, a fan of the earlier Farran, and he recalled several performances he'd particularly enjoyed, while not departing from his required impartiality about politicians—they were all, in his view, "a lot of twisters." He asked me, among other things, if I was often recognized in the street,

and whether it bothered me, and I told him the truth—
that one disliked being recognized and hated not to be.
We chatted, in a desultory way, for nearly half an hour—
our talk punctuated by a couple of telephone calls, which
Fairlie dealt with. Then Davey returned. "The Commissioner would like to see you, Mr. Farran," he said. Just
like that, short and crisp.

I followed him through the corridors, not without some
trepidation. It was what I'd asked for, but the nearer to
the top I got in this improbable affair and the greater
my involvement became, the harder it would be to withdraw. I did hope they realized that it was all quite tentative. . . .

The Commissioner, Sir Keith Boland, was at his desk.
As I'd noted at the Equity dinner, he was a burly man
in his mid-fifties, a no-nonsense, down-to-earth Yorkshire-
man, with the deceptively quiet manner of so many senior
police officers. He said "Good afternoon," indicated a chair
for me, and invited Davey to sit. Then he gave me a long,
searching look, a head-to-foot examination.

"Well, Mr. Farran, I've been hearing about this remarkable suggestion of yours. I can't say I see much resemblance
between you and Lacey." He took a record card from a
file on his desk and passed it to me. "That's how the fellow
looked just after his arrest."

There were two police photographs, full-face and profile.
They were far from studio portraits, but the detail was
much sharper than in the newspaper pictures I'd seen,
and I studied them with interest. Just as, I was aware,
Boland was continuing to study me.

Finally I said, "I agree he's hardly my identical twin,
sir. Not at the moment . . . But the most obvious difference
could be an advantage. The beard and mustache hide a

lot of the face. They could be exactly copied. So could the curly hair style."

"He may have had his beard shaved off and his hair style changed," Boland said.

"That wouldn't matter. This is how his friends last saw him. This is how they'll remember him."

Boland nodded. I had a feeling he'd been testing me—checking up on my IQ.

I glanced through the personal details that accompanied the photographs. "The measurements raise no problems," I said, "He's five feet ten; I'm five nine and a half. He weighed at this time ten stone twelve. I weigh eleven stone. He looks about my build. And the gray-blue eyes are confirmed. . . . Of course, I'd need to know much more." I had to keep on saying that, however tedious the repetition sounded.

"What exactly would you need to know?" Boland asked.

"Well—the way he talks, of course. The quality of his voice. The sort of expressions he uses. The way he walks, the way he sits, the gestures he makes, his mannerisms. His body marks and physical peculiarities, if any. His state of mind, so far as it's known. His interests. His prison routine. And lots of other things. I'd have to work at him until I could feel that I *was* Lacey."

"H'm . . . It would mean an on-the-spot study, of course."

"Oh, yes."

"How long do you suppose you'd need for that?"

"Provided everything was laid on for me, I'd probably be able to tell you in two or three days whether I could do a convincing impersonation."

"I see. . . . Well, Mr. Farran, you won't be surprised to hear that I'm extremely skeptical. I'm not questioning

35

your professional competence—far from it—but at the moment I just can't see it as a practical proposition. Of course, as I'm sure you appreciate, the decision won't be mine—it will have to be taken at the very highest level."

"I realize that."

"Now if, by any remote chance, your suggestion was not turned down out of hand, it seems to me there'd be three major matters to explore. First, whether Mr. Morland would be prepared to pay you the kind of—er—fee that you have in mind if your plan succeeded. Second, whether you could in fact impersonate Lacey with any possibility of success. Third, whether exchange arrangements could be made that would be acceptable to both parties. How do you feel about the priorities?"

"I think your order is right, sir. An agreement about the money would obviously have to come first." Suddenly it was as though John Borley were tugging at my elbow. "And of course I'd want some sort of written contract with Mr. Morland."

"Always a wise precaution! Would you expect an advance?"

"No, just a guarantee. Perhaps a modest sum for expenses, as I'm almost broke. . . . Then I'd do my study of Lacey. That would fit in quite well. As I understand it, the authorities have nine days—eight days now—to decide what to do. If I couldn't satisfy them by then that I could impersonate Lacey successfully, they'd be no worse off than they are at the moment. If the first stage went smoothly, they could move on to the transfer details."

The Commissioner gave a brief nod. "Well, I have your telephone number, Mr. Farran. I don't imagine anything will come of this, but I'd be obliged if you would stay by your phone for the next twenty-four hours."

"I'll do that," I said.

Boland got up and shook hands, which I thought was very courteous of him, and I left with Davey.

12

On the way back to Pimlico, I bought an evening paper and shopped for beer, cigarettes, and food. Then I settled down in the flat to await developments—if any. There was no fresh kidnap news in the paper. The police still had no line on the gang or the whereabouts of Sally Morland; and Downing Street was saying nothing. Frank Morland, understandably, was refusing to be interviewed, and Sally's father, caught in transit by newsmen, had also declined to comment on the situation.

There was a feature article on an inside page, marginally related to the gang's activities, about how easy it was to steal cars for crime. Nothing very new about that, of course, but the quoted figures astonished me: 250,000 taken in the United Kingdom in a single year, the article said, and more than a tenth of them never heard of again. Many of them were undoubtedly used for violent crime—robberies, holdups, and the like—before being dumped. The main cause of the steadily mounting crime rate was the invention of the wheel. . . .

I put the paper aside, watched an old television film, fixed myself a ham omelette for supper, and watched more television, with little concentration.

Once again, I slept only fitfully. I suppose that subconsciously I was listening for the telephone—though by now

I hardly knew whether I wanted it to ring or not. You can get pretty cold feet in the night, even in eighty degrees Fahrenheit. I lay there wondering if Boland had taken any steps yet—and if he had, whom he'd talked to. First, presumably, to his immediate boss, the Home Secretary. Then, perhaps, to the Prime Minister. I'd always understood it was the P.M. who had direct responsibility for security—and the Morland kidnapping was surely a security matter. Perhaps my suggestion wouldn't go beyond those two. I hoped not. Secrecy was obviously vital if anything was to come of it, and full Cabinets often leaked like sieves. . . .

Or perhaps Boland, on reflection, had decided not even to raise the matter. . . .

There was no telephone call during the night, and none next morning. I felt disappointed, relieved, deflated, all sorts of things—though in the light of a new day I wasn't greatly surprised. My idea must have seemed pretty far-fetched to hardheaded men; and asking for a quarter of a million pounds would hardly have endeared me to anyone. Logical, maybe, but not exactly realistic. If *I'd* been in the hot seat, I'd probably have turned the whole idea down flat. Penniless actor—grasping fellow—all talk and no experience of criminals—really, a piece of cheek. . . .

All the same, by midafternoon I began to wonder what was going on. It shouldn't have taken them all this time to come up with a simple no. And how long was I expected to stay cooped up in the flat beside a silent telephone? Had they forgotten about me? It was all getting rather irritating. . . . Then the phone rang, and it was Davey on the line. Would I please come and see the Commissioner at 5 P.M.?

There was no waiting this time. A large man evidently posted as lookout at the reception desk identified me in a split second and escorted me at once to Boland's office. The Commissioner had Davey with him there. They both shook hands with me in a no-time-to-waste manner. I had a tingling sensation of action about to start—and I was right.

Boland said, "Well, Mr. Farran, your suggestion's been discussed, and the decision is that a feasibility study should be made at top speed. I take it you've had no change of mind?"

"Indeed, no."

"Good . . . Mr. Morland has been put in the picture, and he'd like to meet you personally. He's in the building now. He's not in very good shape, as you can imagine, so when he joins us I suggest we try to keep the proceedings as brief as possible."

That suited me. The idea of a long chat with a man whose wife might soon be tortured to death was unappealing. Indeed, I was a little surprised that he should have shown up at all—though politicians, even distressed ones, do tend to show up. Like actors, they move instinctively toward the center of the stage.

Boland spoke into the intercom on his desk, and almost at once Morland was ushered in. He was a big, impressive man, well over six feet and broad in proportion, and he was even more strikingly handsome than his pictures had suggested, though at present his good looks were somewhat ravaged. He had dark shadows under his eyes, which in other circumstances I might have put down to dissipation but which were now clearly the result of sleepless anxiety.

Boland introduced me, and we all sat down.

Morland gazed hard at me for a moment. Then he said, "Well, I've been told of your suggestion, Mr. Farran. . . ." He had a deep, resonant voice, which any professional actor would have envied. "And I appreciate it. The main reservation in my mind is that I don't much care for the idea of asking a man to risk his life on my behalf for money. If anything happened to you—well, I'd feel very guilty."

I said, "But you didn't ask me, Mr. Morland. It was I who made the approach, and I'm prepared to take full responsibility for the consequences—whatever they may be. You already have more than enough to worry about."

He gave a brief nod. "That's true. And, to be honest, I don't feel I've any choice. So I accept your offer, and your conditions. I'll pay you a quarter of a million pounds if your plan goes through and my wife is—returned to me unharmed." His face quivered, and for a moment I thought he was going to break down. It seemed an inappropriate time, in the middle of money talk, and I couldn't escape the feeling that he was hamming it up a bit. I was surprised, too, that he hadn't tried to beat me down over the payment; I thought all tycoons did that. I felt slightly ashamed, as though I were taking unfair advantage of a man's despair.

Still, I wasn't ashamed enough to suggest a reduction. After all, he could well afford it. So all I said was "Fine."

"I understand that you'd like a written contract."

"I would, yes."

"Sir Keith tells me that, for security reasons, he'd prefer the contract to be drawn up and signed in this office, and then kept here under lock and key. Is that acceptable to you?"

"Perfectly."

And I understand you need something for expenses. What sum do you suggest?"

"Would a thousand pounds be too much?"

"I'll write a check now."

Boland said, "I think it would be better if you made it out to the Metropolitan Police, Mr. Morland—and we'll provide the cash. Just a precaution."

Morland nodded. "Of course." He wrote out a check and gave it to Boland. Then he jotted down something on the back of a card, and passed it to me. "I don't expect you'll need to contact me, Mr. Farran, but just in case, this is my ex-directory phone number. . . . And now, gentlemen, perhaps you'll excuse me." He got up and held out his hand to me. His grip was firm. "If your plan ever gets off the ground, Mr. Farran—good luck to both of us!" It wasn't a bad exit line. Not for a man in mental torment.

The atmosphere eased appreciably after he'd gone. The interview had passed off smoothly enough, thanks to Boland's thorough preparation, but it had still been a strain; and the Commissioner turned with obvious relief to the next business.

"I'm going to introduce you now, Mr. Farran," he said, "to the man you'll be working with on the feasibility study." He spoke into the intercom again. "Ask Mr. Smith to come in, will you?"

Mr. Smith came in. He was a tall, lean, wiry-looking

man of fifty or so, with a bronzed complexion and bright blue eyes. He had a silvering toothbrush mustache, and silvering hair at his temples. He was sprucely dressed in a lightweight suit with a rose in the buttonhole, a bow tie, and a white shirt with immaculate cuffs that showed an inch or so of brown sinewy wrists. His shoes of chestnut leather had a mirror gloss. Incredibly, he carried a rattan cane. If I'd been looking for someone to play a retired colonel from the White Highlands, I'd have considered the search over.

Boland said, "Mr. Farran. Mr. Smith," and we shook hands.

"You'd better call me George," Smith said. He glanced at his watch. "The pubs are just opening. Let's go and have a drink."

14

He knew precisely where he was going. He guided me round a couple of corners and steered me into a large saloon. It was almost empty of customers, and there was no one behind the bar. He tapped lightly on the counter with his cane, and at once a barmaid appeared.

"What'll you have?" he asked me.

"Bitter, please."

He raised an eyebrow, and ordered two pints. "I thought your tipple was Scotch," he said.

I stared at him. "What makes you say that?"

"My dear boy, you don't imagine you haven't been vetted, do you? How innocent can you get? We've had a whole posse on the job. . . . By and large, you got good marks. An alpha, I'd say. An alpha minus, anyway . . . There was just this small doubt about your drinking habits."

"I drank," I said, "because I was fed to hell and I'd nothing else to do. That's the only reason. I'm not an addict. I don't even *like* Scotch—it was just the quickest pain-killer. From now on, I assure you, you don't have to worry. It'll be beer or nothing."

"Good . . . Shall we sit down?"

We took our pints to a corner. George laid his cane carefully on a bench and hitched up his trousers to preserve their knife-edge crease before he sat. "Well, cheers!" he said. His blue eyes locked on to me. "You seem a pleasant young fellow, Bob. May I give you a word of friendly advice—unofficial advice? Just between ourselves."

I shrugged. "I'm always ready to listen to advice. What is it?"

"Give up the whole idea," he said. "For the outside chance of a quarter of a million pounds, it's not worth it. These boys would discover you weren't Lacey and they'd tear you apart. If you're bent on suicide, do it comfortably. Throw yourself off Beachy Head."

I laughed. Working with George promised to be stimulating. I said, "I don't agree they'd discover I wasn't Lacey. Not necessarily."

"Then you're living in a dream world. . . . Look—this gang have worked closely with Lacey as a partner. They're buddies of his. They know him intimately. Do you seriously think they could be persuaded when they saw you—however well you were made up—that you were their dear old pal?"

"It would depend entirely on the circumstances," I said. "They might be. After all, it's well over a year since any of them saw Lacey. People can change a lot in a year. Particularly, I should think, when they've spent the year in prison."

"Nobody changes that much. Would *you* mistake a made-up stranger for an intimate friend—after one year? At close quarters and in broad daylight? I just don't believe it."

"Perhaps not in broad daylight," I conceded. "That would be expecting rather a lot. . . . But I've been thinking about this. *Would* the exchange be made in broad daylight? I'm looking at it from the gang's point of view. In daylight it would be much easier for the police to get on their track once the transfer was made. Why should they take the risk? At night they'd have a much better chance of a clean getaway. Of course, one can't know what's in their mind—we'd have to see what happened, what their proposals were. But it does seem to me they'd prefer to operate under cover of darkness. If that happened, they certainly wouldn't realize I wasn't Lacey. In the dark all cats are gray, as the French say."

George looked at me as though, against all expectations, I had come up with a useful thought.

"Well, you may have a point there," he agreed. "Even so, darkness doesn't last forever. What about morning light?"

"I'd hope to be away long before that," I said. "As I see it, they'd either rumble me from the start, which would be just too bad for me, or they'd completely accept and trust me as one of themselves. In which case, it shouldn't be too difficult to give them the slip."

"H'm . . . All right. You're making a lot of assumptions—but let's suppose for a moment they all prove justified. You've been accepted as Lacey in the dark, and before morning you've managed to escape. Where does that leave you? How do you think they'd feel about you? When they'd discovered that they'd been duped, that their hostage was gone and their mate was still in jail? Don't you suppose they'd be after you for revenge?"

"No doubt they would," I said, "in spirit. But as they wouldn't know who I was, they wouldn't be able to do anything about it. . . . Obviously my identity would have to be kept a close secret."

"Someone might give the secret away. Have you thought of that? Someone often does, you know. At the end of the day, a lot of people are going to know about your part in the affair. And things leak out—especially where politicians are concerned. I've been in the secrecy business long enough to know that. If your plan worked, the pressures would be enormous to discover your name. And— in the strictest confidence, of course—someone would murmur it. Fleet Street would hear of it. . . . Then, to be safe or even fairly safe, you'd need permanent police protection. You might even have to change your name, go into hiding. . . . I repeat, dear boy, is it worth it?"

I said I thought it was. What might happen *afterward* seemed too far away to be worth bothering about. "Anyway," I said, "with a quarter of a million pounds stashed away I could probably bear to change my name and start a new life. The old one hasn't been so marvelous. . . ."

George shook his head in what appeared to me to be studied sorrow. "Well—I think you're on a loser, whichever way it goes."

"Somebody must be more hopeful," I said. "Otherwise we wouldn't be starting a feasibility study."

"We're studying the feasibility of a successful exchange—not of your survival afterwards. As far as our political masters are concerned, you're expendable. You're what the Americans call a fall guy. If the exchange goes through, and you survive the aftermath, well and good—they'll take the credit. If the exchange goes through, and you're then rumbled and brought slowly to the boil in a cauldron, too bad. They'll probably give you a citation—but you'll be a dead hero, like your old man."

The expendability angle was one I hadn't considered. I considered it now.

"You may be right," I said after a pause. "All the same, I think I'll take the chance."

"Well, it's up to you. . . . But when they're driving splinters up your nails, don't blame me. I've done my private duty." George took a draught of beer, and wiped his mustache with a silk handkerchief. "So now to my public duty. There'll be a bit of paperwork—but that can wait till tomorrow."

"Paperwork?"

"Official Secrets Act. The powers-that-be will want your signature on the dotted line. Just a formality—you only sign your soul away for life. We all have to do it. . . ." Suddenly he became serious. "Let me tell you the present position about Lacey. Background stuff. He's in Kilhurst jail in Berkshire—a pretty antiquated convict prison, but nice and handy for us. An hour ago I had a talk with the Governor. His name's Wallace—Major Wallace. It seems that immediately he heard the news about Mrs. Morland, and the kidnappers' terms, he took Lacey off all communal activities—work parties, classes, evening association—and put him in solitary."

"Why?"

"Well, a prison isn't hermetically sealed against the outside world. Far from it. They have radio and television. People come and go. News spreads quickly. The view was that Lacey would become restive if he learned what had happened. And other prisoners might give trouble if he were around. Men involved in threats to torture attractive young women to death aren't necessarily popular in jail. They tend to get bashed, like child rapists. You could call it a precautionary measure. . . . Anyway, that's the position. Lacey doesn't know, and won't be told, anything at all about the kidnapping. . . . Now, what's your plan of study?"

"First I'll need to hear him talk," I said. "And to watch him closely, for quite a long time. The longer, the better."

"Yes . . . Well, an interview could easily be set up, of course. In the Governor's office—in Lacey's cell—anywhere. Question and answer . . . But I gather he's not at all forthcoming, and with a stranger asking the questions he could be even more difficult. Obviously it would be much better if you could study him when he was off guard. . . ." George pondered. "Look, how would a video tape and sound track do?"

"It would do very well," I said, "if the recording was good. What are you thinking of?"

"There's a prison visitor—one of these voluntary chaps. A spare-time do-gooder named Mark Grenfell. A caring man. You know—help the killers and forget the killed. He sees Lacey once a week for about half an hour. . . . Suppose we could fix things up in a couple of adjoining cells—Lacey and the visitor in one, closed-circuit television in the other. A hole knocked through the wall somewhere high up for the Magic Eye. I'm not an electronics expert, but I wouldn't think it would be too difficult to get a tape. You could then run it through at your leisure, as often as you wanted. How does that appeal to you?"

The cool way George proposed to knock holes in one of H.M. Prisons was quite breathtaking. I said, "Are you serious?"

"Oh, yes. I think it could be managed."

"Would the prison visitor be told?"

"Good heavens, no! If he knew what was going on, it would be bound to cramp the conversation. I'm sure you'd want everything to be as natural as possible."

"I just wondered. . . . Well, if you think you can work it, it would be ideal."

"Then I'll look into it."

"Of course," I said, "I'd need to see Lacey in the flesh as well. Walking, moving around—exercising, perhaps."

George nodded. "I shouldn't think there'd be any problem there. What else?"

"I'd want a sample of his hair—and beard, if he still wears one. Someone will have to match the color and texture."

"H'm . . . A bit tricky, that one. I suppose he has to have a trim now and again—but I wouldn't want to ask the regular prison barber to collect samples. It might start a train of thought. These fellows are pretty discreet, but they're not Trappists and they mostly have wives. . . . I'll think about it, and work something out. Anything more?"

"I think I ought to look over the prison, in case I'm ever asked about it. Those parts that Lacey would have seen. And I'll need answers to a lot of general questions about him. I'll probably need to see the prison doctor, the visitor you've just mentioned, perhaps the Chief Prison Officer, maybe the chaplain—"

George stopped me. "Hold on, now. The last thing we want is for word to get around the prison that a young man is doing a close-up on Lacey. The fewer people you meet, the better. I suggest you make a list of the questions you have in mind, and we'll ask the Governor to gather the answers. He can do it discreetly—and *he'll* have to know what's in the wind, anyway. . . . With luck, we might be able to get everything over in one short, sharp visit."

I saw his point, and nodded agreement.

"Right," George said. "Then you prepare your list of questions as soon as you get home, and I'll have it sent to the Governor by road this evening. One of my men will wait upon you at eight o'clock. And I'll advise Wallace that it's on the way. How's that?"

"It's unbelievable. You're a real Mr. Fixit, aren't you?"

George smiled a wintry smile. "A little brief authority, that's all. Just a matter of being in with the right people." He fitted a cigarette with a cardboard end into a long holder, an undoubted affectation. "I remember a story someone told me once about a foreigner who got into trouble in some remote part of Russia in the time of the Red Czar, Uncle Joe. Trouble with the security chaps—the Ogpu, they were called then. They opened his luggage, and the first thing they came across was a cabinet photograph of Joe Stalin, inscribed in his own fair hand, 'To my dear comrade Gregori Falk, with all good wishes. Joseph.'"

"What happened?"

"They laid on a banquet for Gregori, and the miscreant who had opened the luggage was dispatched to a labor camp. . . . Of course, the story could be apocryphal."

"Am I to gather that you have someone's photograph in *your* luggage?"

"Not exactly—but the principle's the same." George

glanced at the door as two customers came in, making at least nine of us in all. "I think we'd better make a move," he said. "It's getting crowded in here! By the way, feel free to get in touch with me about anything at any time. There's a round-the-clock service at this number, and wherever I am I can be contacted. Just ask for George." He tore a fragment from the margin of a discarded newspaper lying beside him and wrote the number down. "Think you can remember it?"

I smiled. "I can remember my lines in a three-act play. So I guess I can manage a phone number."

"Good! Sometime, dear boy, you might need it badly— and when you do, there'll be no prompter!" He recovered the sliver of newspaper from me and burned it in an ashtray. "Routine," he said. "Ridiculous, really . . . Now I suggest you get back to Pimlico and do your homework."

15

I took a taxi to the flat and went straight to work on the list. George hadn't allowed me a lot of time, but I'd already considered in detail what I needed to ask about Lacey, and in half an hour I'd produced a fairly comprehensive questionnaire. The items, jotted down as they'd occurred to me and not in any special order of importance, went like this:

1. Has Lacey had any private visitors while in jail? If so, who?
2. Has he sent or received any letters or other communications? If so, details?

3. Has he any body marks or disfigurements that would be noticeable when he's dressed?
4. What has been his general attitude in prison? State of mind? Behavior?
5. Has he shown any special interest in anything? Hobbies, books, games, etc.?
6. What kind of work has he been doing? What sort of pay has he received? How has he spent it?
7. Does he smoke? If so, has he a favorite brand?
8. Has he said anything at all about his fellow payroll robbers?
9. Has he said anything at all about his earlier life? Place of birth? Parents? Education? Pre-gang occupation? Where lived, etc.?
10. Has his health been good? Details?
11. Would it be possible for me to see a sample of his handwriting?
12. Have his own clothes and effects been kept?
13. Could I be given a brief outline of his daily routine in prison prior to the kidnapping—getting up, mealtimes, work schedule, exercise periods, classes, recreation, etc.?

I sealed the list in an unaddressed envelope, with only minutes in hand. Sharp at eight o'clock there was a ring at the door. A man wearing a crash helmet said, "Mr. Farran? I'm from George."

I handed over the envelope. "I expect you've had full instructions. . . ." Considering he was from George, it was a fairly inane remark.

"I have," he said. "Good night, sir." He departed briskly, and a moment or two later I heard his motorcycle roaring away. Top speed had been ordered, and top speed it was.

16

The next thirty-six hours were comparatively unevent-
ful as far as I was concerned—but George was extremely
active. He telephoned me around noon on the following
day to say that he'd been at Kilhurst prison, had had a
long talk with the Governor (who was already working
on my list), and had been given the assurance of maximum
cooperation in our various ploys. All the arrangements
we'd discussed, he said, were now in train. Shortly after
lunch he came to my flat with the "paperwork"—still not
concealing his view that if I continued on my present
course I was unlikely to survive long enough to reveal
any secrets, official or otherwise—and I signed where he
said. I couldn't quite decide whether his repeated warnings
were designed to scare me off or to test my resolution.
On the whole, I thought probably the latter—and that it
was a deliberate part of the feasibility study.

In the afternoon I was summoned to the Yard. There
Davey handed me £1,000 in notes for my expenses (in
return for a receipt) and showed me the undertaking that
Morland had already put his name to and that a police
lawyer had witnessed. It consisted of no more than a single
paragraph, uncomplicated by fine print and clear beyond
question. If, as a result of my impersonation of Tom Lacey,
Mrs. Morland was freed alive, Morland would pay me
£250,000 within two days of that event. Davey said he
would see that the document was safely locked away from
human sight. I left his office in a mood bordering on eupho-

ria. I was hardly able to believe in my potential good fortune. Admittedly the money had to be earned, and I'd no illusions that it would be easy—but that quarter of a million was going to be a very strong incentive in the days ahead.

The thought did cross my mind on the way home that the number of people who knew all or something about what we were up to was growing rather fast. There was Frank Morland, Davey, Boland, George (and probably others in whatever section of Intelligence he served), the prison Governor, the police lawyer, and—if not the whole Cabinet—certainly the Home Secretary and the Prime Minister. And so far we were only at the start of the project. I consoled myself with the somewhat irrelevant thought that a lot of people must have known beforehand about the Normandy landings!

17

Next morning the phone rang while I was shaving. It was George—who else?—saying he would be picking me up at nine o'clock sharp, and that we were going to the prison. He arrived on the dot in a chauffeur-driven car of reasonably modest appearance, and we set off at once for Berkshire. On the way, I told him that Morland had signed the agreement. He nodded, as though he knew all about it, and said with gloomy relish, "Blood in the bank, dear boy." But basically he was quite cheerful, and during the rest of the forty-mile journey we chatted mainly about the theatre, in which he had suddenly developed an acute interest. He asked me, with patent guile, if my job had ever involved dealing with unexpected crises, and I told him about ad-libbing when a fellow actor dried, which seemed to fortify him. I also told him, to pass the time, about my first-ever stage appearance. It had been in a school play—and I remembered the title—*The Hunchback*, by Sheridan Knowles. My simple role had been to go on stage as a messenger and say "Here is the scroll, sire," but in my excitement I'd omitted to take the scroll with me. So I'd had to retreat slowly to the wing, flapping a hand agitatedly behind me once I was out of view of the audience, until some alert youth had thrust the scroll into it. It was a bit of light conversational relief, no more, before we suddenly faced the grim reality and demanding tasks of the jail.

We came to a halt in front of a castellated gatehouse, Scottish baronial or something very like it. Our chauffeur got out and pressed a brass button sunk in stone. There were distant footfalls, followed by the sharp rattle of keys. A wicket gate opened and a uniformed officer appeared. Very courteous. He was, of course, expecting us, and he barely glanced at the credentials George produced before admitting us to the gatehouse. Doors clanged behind the car. Without delay we were passed through an iron grille that formed the opposite end of the gatehouse, and emerged into the prison yard. I'd never been in a prison before, and I gazed around with somber interest. Tall blocks of buildings radiated out from the center in a kind of starfish pattern. To our right there was a wing of fewer stories, which turned out to be the administrative section. Our chauffeur settled himself in the car, opening a newspaper, while George and I were escorted through a glazed door and along a corridor to the Governor's office.

Major Wallace received George with marked respect, and myself with friendly curiosity. He was a man in his middle forties, black-haired, very masculine, very alert. He might, for all I knew, spend most of his time immersed in paperwork and administrative detail, but outwardly he looked the confident disciplinarian on top of his difficult job. In a prison brawl, I felt, he'd have been there on the spot, taking charge, talking the troublemakers down, doing his fearless duty. In short, an impressive man.

After the initial exchanges were over, Wallace suggested I might care to take a look at Tom Lacey right away. It was a convenient time, he said, for the man's morning exercise. He spoke briefly to someone on his office intercom, and presently conducted us along a succession of corridors to a window, which he opened. Below us, there were rectangular plots of sooty turf, with concrete paths around and between them. This, apparently, was one of the exercise areas, and the window gave us an excellent view of it.

In a few moments Lacey was brought out, escorted by two prison officers. There was no mistaking him, for he still had—I was glad to see—his very individual reddish-brown beard and mustache. He was wearing a jersey, shorts, and rubber shoes, and he went at once into a smart walk round the perimeter of the yard. The first thing that struck me as he passed below was the pallor of his face—a pallor rare outside of jail in this grilling summer. I made a mental note that I must keep out of the sun from now on. I'd never pass as a released convict if I showed up with a fine tan.

After a turn or two round the track Lacey started to jog—making one full circuit at a run, the next at a brisk walk. He looked in good physical shape, moving lightly on his feet. I was too far away to be able to study his features, but at this stage that wasn't necessary. It was his general bearing I was concerned with, his stance when he paused briefly in a beam of sunlight and wiped the sweat from his face with his forearm, and the rhythm of his movements. It took an effort to believe, as I watched him from above, that here was a ruthless, trigger-happy murderer starting a life sentence, which in his case could well *mean* life. There was certainly nothing broken-spirited about his appearance; he could have been an eager athlete training for a medal. I continued to observe him closely as he did a little shadowboxing and some skipping—perhaps for fifteen minutes in all. Then I indicated that I'd seen all I needed to of the man in motion, and we returned to Wallace's room.

18

Back in the office, we exchanged a few comments on Lacey's more obvious physical characteristics. Then Wallace produced my list of queries, and we seated ourselves at a small boardroom-type table where I could make notes.

"Well, now, Mr. Farran," Wallace said, "several of your questions can be answered very briefly, and I'll deal with those first. Lacey hasn't had any private visitors since he was brought here, and he hasn't asked for any. Nor has he sent or received any letters. As far as we can tell, therefore, he's had no communication with his former friends. He's remained absolutely silent about the gang he was involved with, and he's refused to say anything about his life before jail. So we're still completely in the dark about his background. The chaplain has approached him once or twice, with entirely negative results. He's been seen occasionally by one of our social workers, and he's been visited regularly by Mr. Grenfell, with whom he has a good relationship on a superficial level. But there have been no confidences at all. I doubt if we've ever had a less communicative prisoner. . . .

"You ask about his general attitude and state of mind in prison. That's a difficult one, since we've had so little to go on. As you'd expect, he doesn't fall into any of the more usual categories." Wallace became professional and discursive. "We have prisoners who suddenly get emotional and pour out their troubles into any willing ear; prisoners who try to justify their crimes and say the court was unfair to them; despairing prisoners who sob on their beds and maintain that life is over; hysterically religious prisoners; hardened prisoners who consider an occasional 'lagging' all in the day's work. . . . Lacey isn't like any of these. He's given no trouble of any sort, physical or psychological. His behavior has been exemplary. Naturally he's shown no remorse for what he did, in view of his professed beliefs, but he's shown no resentment over his treatment either. From the beginning he's seemed remarkably detached and unworried. Self-contained, calm, apparently quite unconcerned about his life sentence. . . . Almost as though he knew that before long his fellow gangsters would make a bid to get him out."

A percipient remark, I thought. It could well be true—and I made a mental note to remember it.

"You ask about his interests," Wallace went on. "Well, he reads a good deal in his leisure time—sometimes works of philosophy and history, well popularized, though he chiefly enjoys straight adventure stories. He's far from being an intellectual, but within limits he's an intelligent and educated man. He had the nerve, a couple of months ago, to ask Grenfell if a special book could be obtained for him—a work called *Fields, Factories and Workshops*, by Peter Kropotkin, another of his nineteenth-century heroes. Grenfell was rather in favor—he had a notion that if they could discuss it together, the dialogue might lead to an eventual change of heart on Lacey's part. However, I didn't feel it was any part of my job to encourage a prison seminar in anarchism, so I turned the application down."

"Quite right," George said irreverently. "You can never be sure who will convert whom!"

Wallace allowed himself a thin smile.

"Has Lacey any other special interests?" I asked.

"Apart from reading," Wallace said, "his main leisure interest has been chess. He sits alone, working out problems. I gather he's a good player, indeed a very good one, and he plays a running game with Grenfell, who's also good, at their weekly meetings. A few moves each time . . ."

I made a note that I must find out something about chess, which was almost a closed book to me.

Wallace glanced down at my list. "Now—health. Lacey's general health has been excellent. He's a fit man who enjoys exercise, and he's in very good shape. It seems he's a little deaf in his left ear—the result of a perforated drum—but it doesn't appear to bother him much. The prison doctor asked him if someone had let off a gun too close to him!—but, as usual, Lacey wasn't to be drawn. Otherwise, no defects . . . Oh, he has one body mark that would show if he were lightly dressed—a large brown mole, roughly the size of a new penny piece, on the outside of his right forearm about nine inches above the wrist. Apart from that, there's nothing that would catch the eye. . . . Smoking? Yes, he does smoke, but only occasionally. When he does, it's always Diplomat cigarettes. . . . The general view is that he's a man of naturally abstemious habits. Our resident psychiatrist tells me that often goes with political fanaticism. . . .

"His work in prison? Well, he's been attached to several work parties. He's good with his hands, and he's done well in the machine shop, and at carpentry. He earns something over a pound a week, which mostly goes on cigarettes. . . . Recently he was making children's rocking horses. At his own suggestion, which was approved, he took to carving chessmen as a sideline—Staunton design, I believe—which has turned out quite profitably for us. Usually we tend to make a small loss on our products, I'm afraid. . . .

"Now what else?" Wallace consulted his marginalia. "Ah, yes—his handwriting. I've got a sample here—one of the written applications he made—with his signature. I'd be glad if you could let me have it back when you've finished with it. . . .

"You ask about his clothes and personal effects. He didn't have any personal effects when he was arrested—unless you count his gun!—so that doesn't arise. His clothes and footwear were handed over to the forensic people for possible identification, and I imagine they worked them over so thoroughly that they're no longer serviceable. Anyway, we don't have them."

George said, "So if by any chance Lacey were released in exchange for Mrs. Morland, you'd have to fit him out?"

"I suppose so. If it were left to us, he'd get the standard issue—reach-me-down suit, underclothes, shoes, raincoat, and so on—the basic outfit."

"In that case," I said, "I might have to ask you for a standard set myself."

"We'd be happy to oblige you, Mr. Farran. Just let us know your measurements. . . . Now, is there anything I haven't covered?"

"Only the daily timetable. The prison routine."

"Ah, yes . . . I've prepared a schedule for you—you'll be able to study it at your leisure." He took an envelope from his file and passed it to me.

I said, "Well, I'm most grateful to you for all your trouble, Major. This has been a most useful session."

"I'm glad to be of help, Mr. Farran. . . . Now you'd probably like to take a look at the place you're supposed to have been shut up in for the past twelve months."

19

We went out again through the glazed door and across the prison yard to the entrance of Block B. Wallace rang the bell, and a prison officer admitted us.

At first glance, the interior of the block suggested the hold of a great ship, with the sky visible only through lights in the deck far above. On each side, running the whole length of the hall, were several tiers of cells, built against the outer walls. The upper stories were approached by steel ladders zigzagging up from the central passageway, and then by long steel galleries. The general layout was not unfamiliar, since many films I'd seen had used a similar prison background. What I hadn't been prepared for was the powerful antiseptic smell—carbolic and cleaning polish, overriding less sanitary ones—and the echoing noise, the clanging of iron doors, the clickety-clack of peepholes, the shouted commands of the officers on duty, giving way suddenly to an almost churchlike silence.

We climbed to the third gallery, up steps worn smooth by innumerable generations of prisoners. Wallace pointed out Lacey's cell—B.3.24—but we didn't go inside. Instead he showed us a similar one. It was, I suppose, about twelve feet by seven, and perhaps nine feet high, with walls of lime-whitened brick above a colored dado. Opposite the door there was a heavily barred window high up in the outer wall. I glanced through some printed cards giving information about appeals, petitions, and prison regulations, and made a mental note of the simple furniture, the pipe that ran through the cell for winter heating, the stock of cleaning materials used by the prisoners, and the emergency bell. Wallace then took us to a recess halfway along the landing with a kind of sink and several water closets where prisoners emptied their slops each morning, and he also drew our attention to a wire net spread at first-floor level to frustrate would-be suicides. As we left, there was a sudden outbreak of hammering from the gallery above—where, Wallace told me, some cells had been withdrawn from use for repairs and redecoration. I wondered if the "repairs" had anything to do with George's Magic Eye, but I didn't ask. Prying into George's activities was something I'd decided not to do. When he was ready, he'd tell me.

On the way back to the yard, we looked in at one of the workshops, where I inspected some of the children's rocking horses and the hand-carved chess sets that I was supposed to have made. The prisoners at work there gave us barely a glance; no doubt they were used to visitors, official and otherwise, being shown around. We also took in a kitchen, a laundry, and a recreation space. By then I'd seen as much of the prison as I needed to give a convincing description of the place if I was ever asked about it— and a good deal more than I liked. The horror of a life sentence in such surroundings was almost beyond imagining.

That was the end of my visit. We returned briefly to Wallace's office, thanked him again for his help, and rejoined our patiently waiting chauffeur. It had been a most useful morning—and it had given me much food for thought.

20

On our drive back to town, George and I had what to an eavesdropper might have seemed a rather odd snatch of conversation.

George said, "Well, do you feel you've made progress?"

"Progress, undoubtedly. It's been a most valuable trip."

"You begin to see yourself as Lacey's alter ego?" His tone was teasing.

I said, "I'm on the way—though there are one or two problems. . . . I'm a bit concerned about that mole on his arm."

George said, "I guessed you might be. But if you're still serious about all this nonsense, there shouldn't be any great difficulty. Moles are unsightly and sometimes uncomfortable."

I said, "So?"

George said, "So Lacey could have had his removed in prison. Who's to know he didn't? If you got your forearm cut about a bit in the same spot, in a week you'd have a healed scar and an acceptable story."

I said, "Thanks!"

George said, "You should be grateful for small mercies, dear boy. He could have had a finger missing. Or anything!"

I said, "You're such a comfort, George."

21

Back at the flat, I spent some time thinking over what I had learned at the prison, and what I had failed to learn. One of the conclusions I came to was that, in any impersonation of Lacey, I was going to get little help from an understanding of his psychology and disposition. There just wasn't enough to go on. Even things like his apparent stoicism, his stubbornness, and his silence might be simply his reaction to prison circumstances, and not normally part of his nature. For all I knew, he might be a boisterous and outgiving man with his friends—and if I took the wrong line, there'd be surprise, questions, perhaps danger. . . . Which meant that if I did eventually encounter his fellow gangsters, I'd be wise to lay off extremes of behavior, and rely on voice and outward appearances for the deception. Voice was a matter for the future; but I passed a good hour at the flat that evening consciously recalling Lacey at exercise and practicing his movements—particularly his light-footed walk—while they were fresh in my mind.

I also went carefully through Wallace's "Day in the Life of a Prisoner," and memorized the schedule in case I was ever asked about it. It was certainly no bed of roses. Prisoners rise at 6:30 A.M. Slop out. Clean their cells. Breakfast. Then associated labor for eight hours, with a break for dinner at noon and one hour for exercise sometime during the day. Some form of physical drill for the younger ones. Supper at 5:30 P.M. (Sample of week's menu attached.) Then cells, classes, or recreation. Lights out at 9 P.M. The picture of prison life. In Lacey's case, forever and forever . . . Unless, of course, the authorities weakened and let him go.

22

I slept soundly after my strenuous day at the prison, and woke in a more cheerful frame of mind than I'd known for a long time. Having a job to occupy me—and a greater job in prospect—had given me an enormous lift. Next thing I'd be singing in my bath!

Once again the morning papers had little fresh to report about the kidnapping. The authorities were, naturally, still keeping mum about their intentions, not least because they didn't yet know what their intentions were. The special writers were working over old material in a pretty tired way. Some of the editorials had begun to adopt a needling tone about the Government's supposed indecisiveness. One leading article in a tabloid had the caption "NINE-DAYS WONDER-WHAT-TO-DO," which in all the circumstances I didn't feel was terribly funny.

It wasn't until the late afternoon that I heard from George again. He rang me around four-thirty and said he was on his way to the flat with some "interesting exhibits." He arrived soon afterward, with a briefcase under his arm. There was no mistaking the air of quiet satisfaction in his manner. The news he had to impart was obviously good news.

First he produced an envelope, with two smaller envelopes inside it. "Lock of baby's hair!" he said. "Handle it gently." One of the small envelopes had "Head" written on it. The other had "Beard." I opened them both with care. They contained two small but adequate reddish samples.

"How did you manage it?" I asked.

"Oh, I sent our own *coiffeur* down," George said nonchalantly. "It seemed the best thing in the circumstances. All arranged with Wallace, of course. A talented chap, our barber, and very discreet. You'll be meeting him shortly. . . . He did the job in Lacey's cell. Said he'd come to trim up his beard and hair—Chief Prison Officer's instructions. Said the usual barber wasn't well. Suffering from impetigo, I think he said. Very off-putting. . . . When he'd finished, he gathered up the bits, and that was it."

"Well, that's splendid," I said. Then I had an afterthought. "I suppose this means the Chief Prison Officer is in on the plan now?"

"Not the whole of it," George said. "But he knows there's something in the wind. Wallace has obviously had to take him into his confidence to some extent, with all the strange things that are going on in the jail. I don't think there's any serious risk. The fellow's been in the service for twenty-five years, he's a very reliable man, and he's pledged to silence. . . . Now here's something else the barber got."

George extracted some photographs from his briefcase and passed them to me. They were close-ups of Lacey's hair, in color, taken from the back and from both sides. "He used a Minox," George said, "with a special film. I think they show the style quite well."

I studied them. "Couldn't be better," I agreed.

George put the exhibits back in his case. "Right," he said. "Now we've got some visiting to do."

"Oh? Where are we going?"

"First we'll take these items back to the barber—and get you measured up. He's our disguise man, and he's all set to do a fast job for you. . . . Then we'll take a look at the video tape."

"You've got that!"

"Yes, it was done yesterday evening. I gather all went well."

He had his own car outside, and we were quickly on our way. We drove first to Chelsea, to a small detached house behind the King's Road with a studio on the upper floor. A smiling little man let us in. He was about five feet two, and was almost lost in a paint-stained smock. George introduced him as Harry, and I gave his proffered hand a cautious shake. I was beginning to feel like a campaigning politician with all the glad-handing. Harry took us up to the studio, which at one end was fitted out like a barber's saloon with armchair, basin, mirrors, and the usual instruments. George returned the Lacey hair samples and the photographs, and Harry ran a tape round my head and face in various directions and made a few notes. He hadn't the touch of my favorite TV make-up girl, but he seemed to know his business.

We were off again in a few minutes, this time to a block of flats in St. John's Wood and up in the lift to a penthouse. The man waiting for us there was introduced as Arthur, and there was more handshaking. He was an elderly man, thin, graying, and slightly stooping. In a film he'd have been perfect as a Swiss clockmaker. He already had everything set up for us in his sitting room. There were a couple of well-placed easy chairs opposite a large TV set, and various bits of equipment behind it that presumably had something to do with the show. I was given a gadget that Arthur said would stop the picture at any point I wished, and the black-and-white screen lit up.

23

George's undercover technicians had done a remarkable job. There was a clear view of about half of a prison cell, the half farther from the door. It showed the low bed, backed up against the lime-washed bare brick, with the dado above; an upright wooden chair; a small table; and a chest of drawers. Tom Lacey was sitting on the bed in trousers and a jersey. He had a pad of paper in his right hand, with some squiggles on it, and he kept referring to it as he set out chessmen on a board. Evidently he was preparing to resume an unfinished game. The sound track was perfect; I could even hear the slight thump as the pieces went down. Presently there was the rattle of a key in the door, and a man moved into the picture. Presumably, Mark Grenfell. He was a tall, lanky, balding man, with sloping shoulders on which a jacket of some thin material hung loosely. He looked as though he might be in his late forties. He could have been an accountant or a civil servant or almost anything in the white-collar line. His expression was cheerful and his smile friendly. Lacey got up from the bed, shook hands with him, and said "Hullo, Mr. Grenfell," but he didn't smile in return.

Grenfell said, "So you've changed your address, Tom. They told me so at the gate, but I nearly went into three twenty-four from force of habit."

"They moved me the day before yesterday," Lacey said.

Grenfell glanced around. "Not a lot of difference in the furnishings, eh? . . . The light's an improvement, though."

Lacey nodded. "Someone must have shoved in a big bulb."

"It feels nice and cool here, anyway. Outside it's much too hot for comfort. Well over eighty degrees."

"I could probably put up with it!" Lacey said.

I pressed the gadget and held the picture there. Lacey had an accent. Only a trace—but the clipped speech, the bitten-off words, the flattened vowels were unmistakable. I said, "George, did they ever make inquiries about him in South Africa or Rhodesia?"

"I believe they did," George said. "But they didn't get any line on him."

I nodded, and restarted the tape. Grenfell's static smile was moving again at Lacey's dry remark about being willing to be out in the heat.

"Anyway, Tom, how are you?" he asked.

"I wish someone would tell me why I've been shifted," Lacey said. "And why I'm being kept in solitary. No work to do. No classes. Exercising on my own. What's the big idea?"

"Now you know I can't talk about that, Tom. You don't want to get me struck off the visitors' list, do you? Maybe it won't last too long."

"Couldn't you do something about it, Mr. Grenfell?"

"I could raise it in the usual way. But I don't guarantee results."

"I wish you would," Lacey said. "It's getting on my nerves."

"Well, our game should cheer you up." Grenfell sat down on the hard chair and studied the chessboard. "I seem to remember I'm in a spot of trouble here."

"You are," Lacey said.

"Let me just check the pieces." Grenfell consulted a page in a pocket book. "Yes, that's right. . . . It's your move—and I bet I know what it'll be."

Lacey moved a piece. Grenfell nodded, and replied. Lacey moved again. Grenfell considered. "H'm—difficult."

There was a long pause for reflection. Lacey gazed around the cell, stroked his beard, smoothed an eyebrow, watched Grenfell's face. "We ought to have a time clock," he said as the minutes passed. It was another quip—but he still didn't smile.

Grenfell finally made his move, and the play went on. Both men were concentrating on the game, and there was little talk. Just the odd monosyllable, the odd brief comment.

The tape had been running for a little under half an hour when Grenfell glanced at his watch and pushed back his chair.

"Well, I'm afraid that's our lot for today, Tom." He made a note of the new positions. So did Lacey.

Grenfell got up. "Don't let yourself get too down-hearted," he said. "I'll try and have a word with someone about you. . . . And I'll be back next Tuesday—hopefully to finish you off."

"That's a laugh," Lacey said, shoveling the chessmen back into their box. He got up and shook hands again. "Thanks for coming, Mr. Grenfell. Wish I'd been able to offer you a beer!"

Grenfell passed out of view. There was a clang from the door, the sound of the key turning in the lock, the sound of voices outside—and the tape ended.

George said, "Well, what do you think of it, Bob?"

"Absolutely fine," I told him. "Far better than I expected."

"A bit short on dialogue, perhaps?"

"Yes—but there's enough. . . . Can we run it through again?"

"Of course."

I stopped the tape twice on the second run-through. Once when there was an excellent frontal view of Lacey's hair, mustache, and beard as he gazed directly into the invisible Magic Eye. Once when there was a very good angle shot. "If your friend Harry could have those as stills," I said, "I think he'd be helped a lot with his make-up."

George looked questioningly at the operator. "How about it, Arthur?"

Arthur said, "No trouble, sir. I'll get on to it right away."

I said, "Thanks, Arthur . . . And could I come back here—wherever 'here' is—in the morning? I'll need to run through this tape at least half a dozen times."

"Be our guest," George said. He gave me the address. "I'll be busy myself till lunchtime, but Arthur will look after you. . . . Shall we say ten o'clock?"

24

I was back at St. John's Wood on the dot of ten next day, and I spent three hours with Arthur running through the tape, over and over, until he must have been sick of the sight and sound of it.

I concentrated first on the talk. The exchanges with Grenfell seemed to confirm what Wallace had already indicated—that Lacey was no chatterer. Considering that he'd been living almost entirely incommunicado for several days, it might have been expected that he'd pour words into the visitor's friendly and receptive ear. But no. He spoke only in short sentences—or no sentences at all. "No work to do." "No classes." "Exercising on my own." He was laconic, and probably so by nature. I couldn't imagine him ever holding forth in fluent periods, even to his buddies. I began to readjust my ideas about not trying to portray him in the round. Perhaps this *was* the real Lacey— whom I should aim to impersonate just as he appeared to me.

I noted again the man's dry, throwaway humor—always unsmiling. That would be simple—and important—to copy.

I watched his lips as he talked. I watched how he drew breath. I studied the emphasis and rhythm of his words— something that was almost as individual as fingerprints. As George had said, we could have done with more material, but I thought I could manage. As for the slight accent, it was a gift for any imitator. Colorless speech is naturally hard to copy. Accented speech is easy. With a little practice I knew I'd be sound-perfect. On the second run-through, I taped the track on a pocket recorder I'd brought with me, so that I could work on it at home.

Next I studied the outward look and behavior of the man. His facial expressions and gestures. The way he used his hands. The way he sat. I noted a slight bending of the head, an inclination of the deaf left ear, as Grenfell addressed him. That was a characteristic that would be well remembered by anyone who'd known him.

The only thing that seriously bothered me was a detail of his close-up appearance. The mouth was all right—though I'd have to learn to keep my lips firmly compressed when I wasn't speaking. The nose was all right, give or take a millimeter. An ordinary nose. The ears were all right—no one took much notice of ears unless they were peculiar in size or shape, and his weren't, and neither were mine. But the set of Lacey's eyes was on a slightly upward slant, and the set of mine was dead level. That worried me, because the way eyes are set in their frames of bone and skin enormously affects the expression of a face. And of course it's the expression, as much as the actual contours, that people recall.

When George joined us just before one o'clock and asked me how I'd got on, I told him about the eyes, and gave him a partial rerun of the tape to show him what I meant. I also demonstrated by pushing up the skin beside each of my eyes for perhaps a quarter of an inch.

George seemed unimpressed—even amused. "You're being rather a perfectionist, aren't you—for this stage of the feasibility study?"

"It could be important," I said. "It could make just the

difference between total acceptance and slight uneasiness."

"Well, Dr. Fu Manchu, if necessary I should think it could be fixed. A very minor surgical operation, I'd say. A couple of tucks would probably do the trick. Stitches out in a week. You could have it done at the same time as your mole mark. I know a very good man—very experienced, very discreet, very reliable. . . . But only, of course, if other things seemed to be going well. Personally, I'd wait a bit."

"Time's getting short," I reminded him. "What is it now—four days, or three, before the deadline?"

"Three," he said. "But there's no need to excite yourself, dear boy. I assure you we've plenty of time. First they have to communicate with us again. To learn our decision, as they said. After that, they're bound to allow a day or two for an answer. The mere mechanics of exchanging messages could take quite a while. So let's play it cool, eh? Meanwhile, how about a spot of lunch?"

25

That afternoon, Harry the barber telephoned me. He said he was ready for what he called a "fitting," so I took a taxi to Chelsea straight away. Harry answered the door and I climbed with him to the studio. There he showed me, not without pride, the pieces of human hair he had made up. I had worn, in the course of my job, a great variety of wigs and beards, but never anything of better craftsmanship. These were works of art, and I knew that

Harry must have toiled almost nonstop to produce them in the time.

He put me in the chair opposite the mirror and gave me a short-back-and-sides, so that my own hair wouldn't get in the way. Then he adjusted the wig on my head, referring once or twice to Lacey's pictures. Finally he attached the beard and mustache with the merest touch of spirit gum.

"How's that?" he asked, stepping back.

I studied myself in the mirror. The close wiry curls of the wig were absolutely right. The beard and mustache looked completely natural. The color exactly matched the samples. From the chair, I looked so like Lacey that it was spooky.

I said, "That seems to be just about perfect, Harry."

"Not bad, is it?" He held up a hand mirror behind me so that I could see the back of the head—and that was faultless, too. The curls came just to the nape of the neck, as in Lacey's picture. He said, "You'll need to use more gum, of course, when you take to the trail—but you know all about that. . . . How long do you think you'll be wearing these things?"

It was a pertinent question. I said, "I've no idea, Harry—but I hope only for a few hours. Otherwise they'll get damned uncomfortable."

"Yes—you'll be scratching your head off. . . ." He gave me a last close inspection. "I'll have to touch up your eyebrows before you finally set out. It's a good thing you're blond, not dark—there'll be no difficulty." He eased the hairpieces free, stroked them gently, wrapped them in soft tissue, and placed them in a box. "They'll be here when you need them," he said. "Anytime, day or night. Just give me a ring."

26

I spent much of the evening practicing with my sound-track tape. Going over bits of the dialogue, mostly in front of the mirror, so that I could check the expressions on my rubbery features. I was actually talking to myself and pulling experimental faces when George made one of his increasingly frequent appearances at the flat. As usual, he was well up to date with developments.

"I gather from our friend Harry," he said, "that you're reasonably pleased with his efforts."

"That's an understatement, George. I'm delighted. He's a wonderful craftsman."

"He's had a lot of practice." George's roving glance took in the tape recorder on the table. "How's the mimicry coming along?"

I gave him a short rendering of Lacey's voice. Although he was prepared for it, he looked as startled as Davey had done when I'd imitated the Commissioner. Indeed, he stared at me as though I'd performed some kind of miracle.

"That's very good," he said slowly. "Very good *indeed*."

"You don't have to sound so surprised, George—after all, it is my trade. Would you be surprised at a plumber fixing a washer?"

He grinned. "There are slight differences. . . . Anyway, I'm very impressed."

"You should see me in full fig—beard, mustache, and wig. I practically *am* Lacey."

He looked at me reflectively, as a doctor might appraise the progress of a patient. "Well," he said, "perhaps the time has come for a trial run."

"A trial run?"

"A feasibility study wouldn't be complete without a trial run. . . . Just to see if you really *can* get by—with someone who knows Lacey well."

I dwelt on that. "It would have to be someone from the prison," I said.

"Of course."

"Well, I suppose Wallace would cooperate. He'd probably enjoy giving me the once-over."

"That would be only half a trial," George said. "He'd be expecting you to look like Lacey, and he'd know you weren't. It would be just another opinion—and no better than my own. What we need to do is *deceive* someone."

There was relish in his voice.

I said, "Have you anyone in mind?"

"Well, someone like—Grenfell?"

He sounded as innocent as though the name had come to him by chance out of a hat, but I wasn't taken in.

"What's your plan?" I asked.

"Lock you up in a cell on visiting night. Have Grenfell visit you as Lacey. And see what happens."

I looked at him doubtfully. "Is it practicable?"

"I'd have to go into that with Wallace. Obviously it would take quite a bit of setting up. But I think it could be done."

"Would Wallace play? Making use of an unsuspecting prison visitor who trusted him?"

"He's already done that," George said. "Over the Magic Eye . . . Anyway, if the instruction came from the top he'd have no choice. Reasons of state—overriding considerations."

"Grenfell wouldn't be very pleased if he ever found out."

"Who knows? He'd probably see the necessity when the position was explained to him afterwards—especially if there was an O.B.E. thrown in as a sweetener. . . . But if things went as you seem to think they might, he probably *wouldn't* find out."

"How about the next time he visited the real Lacey? It would be bound to come out then. Lacey would want to know why he'd been missed out last week. . . ."

George shook his head. "No problem there. After he'd seen you, Grenfell would be told that Lacey was to be transferred to another prison. A distant one. End of visits to Lacey."

I had to smile. "You're outrageous, George. Have you no scruples at all?"

He said, "I have my order of priorities, dear boy, and freeing Mrs. Morland from a murderous gang rates higher than a prison governor's loyalty to a visitor, or a prison visitor's hurt feelings. I'll go and see Wallace tomorrow—and if I get the green light, you and I will conspire."

27

We did conspire!

Approximately forty hours later—to be precise, at three o'clock in the afternoon—I was with Harry the barber, who was putting the finishing touches to my appearance. The wig and beard and mustache were already in place, and he was concerned only with my eyebrows, which had to be plucked a little to match Lacey's before they were tinted. He'd been working on me for nearly two hours before he declared himself, as he put it, provisionally satisfied. This, after all, was only the trial run, not the real thing. I arranged with him that I'd be back late in the evening—perhaps very late—to have everything taken off.

George called for me in his own car at five-thirty. By then I was doubly disguised. I was wearing a well-cut suit of clerical gray and a smart, if unfashionable gray hat—a trilby, I think it was called—with a wide brim that turned down at the front. It was just about the first hat I'd ever worn in my life, and it felt very strange—but it usefully covered my wig, and it shadowed the upper part of my face. I also had a pair of heavy horn-rimmed spectacles with plain glass instead of lenses that were a leftover from a show I'd been in. My russet beard was largely concealed by one of those neck or spine supports, rather like a horse collar, which some unfortunates have to wear. A very large, empty briefcase completed my outfit. The purpose of the second disguise, of course, was to make me appear to the ordinary prison staff as a respectable, if somewhat decrepit visitor, who had no resemblance to Lacey.

We drove without incident to Kilhurst, passed through into the prison after the usual brief formalities at the gate, and were once more escorted to the Governor's office. Wallace was a little reserved in manner, but fully cooperative in action. I'd gathered from George that he'd had the expected initial misgivings over the plot, but that these had been dispelled by a personal telephone call from Downing Street. I was introduced to the Deputy Governor, whose name was Jackson—a younger and less military type than Wallace. The number of people who knew about the basic plan was still growing alarmingly, though obviously Jackson couldn't have been kept in the dark about what was going on under his nose. We exchanged a few words, with an eye on the clock, while Wallace brought out a pair of prison trousers—checked for size against a pair of my own that George had borrowed—together with a light prison jacket and a pair of canvas prison shoes, all of which I stuffed into my briefcase. The four of us then set off for Block B. George walked in front with the Governor, Jackson and I brought up the rear. We were quickly admitted in answer to our ring, and continued on up the iron stairway, halting from time to time as Wallace and Jackson, with suitable gestures, appeared to be explaining things to their VIP guests.

We climbed eventually to the top landing, the temporarily unused fourth floor, where there was a strong smell of decorators' paint. On the way, we passed the blue-uniformed, silver-buttoned, white-collared Chief Prison Officer, whose smart salute gave nothing of his knowledge away. Two other officers were on duty in the gallery, and they also saluted smartly. They were George's men, though I wouldn't have known it if I hadn't been told.

Wallace unlocked one of the cells, and we went inside. I changed quickly into prison garb, putting on the light jacket to conceal my lack of a mole on the forearm. I squeezed my hat, my own clothes, my neck support, and my glasses into the capacious briefcase, and the other three left me, taking the case with them. Wallace locked the cell door behind him. I heard them go into the adjoining cell, where my belongings were to be left. Then their footsteps receded, and I was on my own.

I glanced around. The cell had the usual basic furniture—bed, table, chair, chest of drawers, and rudimentary facilities. There was a chess set and board on the table, the same set that Lacey had used, and beside it the pad on which he had noted the state of play when the game was suspended. Ignoring his symbols, which meant nothing to me, I set out the chessmen on the board in the positions that had been faithfully recorded by the TV Magic Eye.

I sat back on the bed, sweating a little. What happened in the next half-hour couldn't hurt me, but I knew that our major plan would probably stand or fall by the result. And the test wasn't going to be just of my appearance and speech. It was also going to be a test of my ability to avoid sudden pitfalls. . . .

I didn't have to wait long. Voices became audible. Grenfell, speaking to one of George's substitute officers. Footfalls sounded along the gallery. A key grated in the lock and the door clanged open. Greenfell fiddled with some bolts and left the door ajar—a routine that I'd been advised was a visitor's required practice. He came forward, smiling. I got up from the bed and shook hands.

"Glad to see you, Mr. Grenfell."

"I'm glad to see you, Tom." He looked around the cell. "I don't know what's happening in this establishment—every time I come I'm given a different number. . . . Well, how are you?"

"Not too good," I said.

He peered at me, concern in his face. And frowned.

"You don't *look* quite yourself. . . ."

For a moment I felt weak at the knees. Was this to be the humiliating end of the trial run—almost before it had started? One close look—and exposure?

Apparently not.

"I do hope it's nothing serious," he said. "Have you asked to see the doctor?"

"I'm not ill," I told him. "I'm just damned fed up. All

this shunting around. Stuck in here most of the day. And the smell of paint's enough to make a guy puke."

"It is rather strong, isn't it? But I'm told the decoration's finished, so it should wear off quite quickly."

"I still don't know why I'm being kept on my own. It's been more than a week now. Did you speak to anyone, Mr. Grenfell?"

"I had a word with the Deputy Governor. It seems there's some big reorganization going on."

A discreet man, Grenfell. A trustworthy man. He knew about the kidnapping, he knew exactly why Lacey was being segregated, he knew that the isolation would continue until the Morland affair was resolved—but never a careless word.

I changed the subject. "At least they still let me read. Could you recommend some more books? Something exciting, to take my mind off things?"

"Well, now, let's see. . . ." Grenfell moved on to less tricky ground with evident relief. "You liked Hammond Innes, didn't you? Have you tried John Buchan?"

"No."

"They're very good adventure stories. A bit old-fashioned, but quite gripping. He had a hero, Richard Hannay, who runs through the series. I think you'd enjoy them. If they're not in the library, I expect some arrangement could be made. . . . I'll find out, shall I?"

"Thanks."

"Now, then, what about our game?" He looked at the board.

I looked at it, too. The distribution of the pieces meant absolutely nothing to me, but someone in George's outfit had studied the position, and I'd been briefed on what to say. "I reckon you might as well resign," I said. "You haven't a hope. Queen takes knight, check, and that's it."

Grenfell nodded. "I'd come to the same conclusion, Tom. So that makes four games to three in your favor. . . . Would you like to start another one now?"

"Not tonight," I said, "if it's all the same to you. I'm not much in the mood. Bit out of sorts. Not enough fresh air." I began to put the pieces back in their box. "What's going on in the big world, Mr. Grenfell? Anything I'm allowed to hear about?"

"Well, now, let me think. . . ." Grenfell started to give me a run-down of some of the lighter items in the day's news. He was, I decided, a most kindly and conscientious man, undoubtedly dedicated to his self-imposed job of cheering up the prisoners on his list. He turned out, surprisingly, to be an armchair cricket enthusiast, and a keen supporter of Surrey. He rattled on for several minutes about various players and their achievements, and though I couldn't imagine that Lacey had ever been a fan of cricket I listened to Grenfell's reminiscences with apparent interest, my left ear cocked in Lacey style to catch his words. By now I was consciously playing out time, and it was a relief when he finally got up to go.

I was alone in the cell for nearly an hour after he'd locked me in and departed. That was to give him time to finish his visits and get clear of the premises. I sat on the bed, thankful that it was all over, a little weary from the effort and strain of the interview, but cheerful. Finally footsteps sounded in the gallery, the door of the adjoining cell opened and shut, and the Deputy Governor came in with my briefcase. I changed back into my somewhat crumpled outfit, substituting the prison clothes, and we made our way down through the block. George's men saluted, and one of them winked at me. The Chief Prison

Officer sedately followed us down. The other officers on duty showed no special interest. Our enterprise seemed to have worked exactly according to plan.

George was with Wallace in his office. Surprisingly, neither of them asked me how I'd fared, as the Deputy Governor had done. So I told them. "It all went without a hitch," I said. "I'm sure Grenfell hadn't the slightest suspicion."

"We know he hadn't," Wallace said. "This has just been brought in. Take a look. . . ." He passed me a notebook. It was Grenfell's visitor's suggestion book. The last entry ran, "Tom Lacey is in low spirits tonight. I think he would benefit from longer exercise periods."

Wallace said, "Congratulations on your performance, Mr. Farran. . . . Let us hope these bizarre activities will prove justified."

28

Though undoubtedly impressed by the outcome of the trial, George still seemed reluctant to take a final view, and I didn't quarrel with that. The success of the experiment had naturally increased my own confidence, but I wasn't yet entirely satisfied. The conditions in the cell had favored me. The light had been adequate, but not bright. A severer test might well lie ahead. The eye problem still worried me—and of course there was the danger of the missing mole. Obviously I couldn't count on keeping my right forearm covered in all circumstances. I discussed the matter again with George, in a rather more serious vein than on the first occasion. As a result, he made an appointment for me at some place he described as a private clinic, and the next afternoon he drove me there. It was out in the country, somewhere in Sussex not far from Lewes. Evidently it was a *very* private clinic, because a big sign warned against unauthorized entry, and there was a guard on the gate.

The staff inside were friendly, matter-of-fact, and uninquisitive. No names were asked for, or given. George had brought along a full-faced picture of Lacey, and I pointed out to the surgeon the slight upward tilt of the eye setting, which I said I would like him to copy as far as possible. He didn't seem at all surprised by the request, and after a brief examination he told me what he proposed to do. He would make an incision on each side of the forehead under the hairline, remove a little skin, and sew up the gap. In fact, put in George's "tuck." With a local anesthetic, he said, the small operation would be quite painless; and the after effects would be negligible. Naturally it would slightly alter my appearance—that being the object of the exercise—but if later I didn't like the way I looked, new skin could be grafted and the operation reversed. As for the missing mole, that was a trifling matter. I said, "Okay— fine," and he led the way into a small operating theatre and, with the assistance of a nurse, got to work.

All went smoothly, and in a little over an hour I was ready to leave. I had a piece of plaster on my right forearm in the spot I'd marked X, and a patch of gauze on each side of my forehead, and that was all. George drove me back to Pimlico, and we had a beer together in the flat. He said he'd be calling again sometime next day, possibly with news, since it was now nine days since Sally Morland's kidnapping, and word in some form could be expected.

My tiny wounds gave me very little trouble overnight.

The arm was a bit sore in the morning, and both my eyes were darkly ringed, but where the skin incisions had been made there was almost nothing to be seen under the gauze except a few neat stitches.

I stayed in the flat all morning, listening to the B.B.C. bulletins. No new developments were reported, but the kidnapping was back in the commentaries in a big way. IS THIS THE DAY OF DECISION? was the theme.

I confess I got quite a kick out of listening to all the talk. When you happen to know more than the pundits, you realize how they waffle.

29

George showed up in the late afternoon, without prior notice. He was carrying a small cassette player, and from the unaccustomed grimness of his manner I judged that he hadn't brought it along for entertainment.

He gave my ringed eyes a perfunctory inspection. "You look as though you were out on the tiles last night! How are you feeling?"

I said I was feeling fine.

"Good." The monosyllable abruptly ended consideration of my health and welfare. George put his machine on the table. "A cassette arrived at the Yard," he said, "by the first delivery today. Posted in Leeds, if that's of any interest. Addressed to the Commissioner, and marked 'Re Sally Morland—Urgent.' I've got a recording of it."

He slipped a cassette into the slot and pressed the start button. There were background sounds. Then a voice with a broad West Riding accent said: "If you agree in principle to the Morland-Lacey exchange, let the B.B.C. broadcast an SOS for Arthur Thompson before the six-o'clock news tonight. Otherwise we shall get to work on Mrs. Morland as already indicated."

I was about to speak, but George checked me. "Wait!"

The voice came on again. "In case you don't believe us, listen to this." There was a short silence. Then another voice said, "Okay—burn her!" And there was a ghastly sound. A sort of muffled scream, as though agony were being half-confined by lips taped together. Then—silence again.

I stared at George in horror. "Christ—that's awful. Really awful . . ."

He nodded. "Blood-chilling, isn't it? By the way, did you notice anything unusual about the background?"

I shook my head. I was still in a state of near shock at the enormity of what I'd heard.

"Listen again to the first part," he said.

I listened. This time I knew what George meant. The background sound *was* unusual. Not exactly a hum or a buzz, but something in between. A sort of susurration. And there was a very slight echo.

"It sounds to me as though someone had left a tap running," I suggested. "In a large empty room."

"It does, doesn't it? The trouble is, there are so many taps, and so many large empty rooms. . . . What do you make of the accent?" He ran the first part of the message through again.

"Phony, I'd guess. Stage Yorkshire. A bit too much of the "Ilkla Moor Baht At" touch . . . Has there been a decision, George?"

"Yes," he said, "there has. After the cassette arrived, I was called to Downing Street to report to the Top Man. He wanted to know what progress we'd made. I told him about your successful trial run at the prison. He was very impressed. He asked for my advice about the next step. Against my personal inclinations, I said I thought the feasibility study should move on to the second stage. In short, that we should find out the proposed exchange terms. . . . The decision is that the SOS should be broadcast."

"Good!" I'd have been surprised—and by now more than disappointed—if the verdict had gone the other way. "What's the public going to be told?" I asked.

"Very little. 'A communication has been received from the kidnappers and is being considered.' Something like that. Noncommittal." George picked up his tape machine. "Well, I've got some chores to attend to. I'll be back later this evening to discuss Stage Two with you. . . . Coddle yourself, dear boy, while you still can!"

Just before six o'clock, I switched on the radio. The announcer said: "Before the news, here is an SOS. Will Arthur Thompson, believed to be touring the West Country in a red Mini, registration number JMD 726 K, telephone his mother in Trondheim, Norway, where his father, Benedict Thompson, is dangerously ill."

I wondered who had thought up that farrago. As though I didn't know . . .

30

When George returned to the flat that evening, it quickly became apparent that what he wanted was not so much a discussion about Stage 2 as a receptive audience while he thought aloud. He looked relaxed enough, sitting comfortably back on my settee in his shirt sleeves—a rare concession to the continuing heat—and drawing on a Russian cigarette through his holder. But he wasn't mentally relaxed. The tension showed in the uncharacteristic stiffness of his language when he began to speak.

"Now that we've reached the run-up to a possible exchange," he said, "I've been thinking about some of the practical aspects of the transaction. The general aspects, which would apply irrespective of the precise terms. I've been thinking of them particularly from the point of view of the gang. And I'm puzzled. What I find very hard to imagine is any kind of exchange operation that would give *them* security."

I said, "Go ahead, George—talk. I'm an innocent in these things."

"Well, there are several points. First, once the exchange had taken place, they'd have—as they'd suppose—Tom Lacey on their hands. A man whose outward characteristics we know in minutest detail, from his mole to his deaf ear to his fingerprints. Obviously he'd shave off his beard and mustache as soon as he could, maybe dye his hair, in fact change his appearance in every possible way. But even so, they'd have to keep him under wraps for quite a time. Not as a prisoner, like Sally Morland—that's comparatively simple—but as a free and equal member of the gang. Where would they do that? What hideout would be secure for long—with publicity nationwide, and everyone in the country on the lookout for the quarry and alerted to report the slightest unusual happening that might be connected with him? There've been such manhunts before—and almost always, in the end, the man has been found. So what makes them think they can get away with it?"

"Go on," I said as he paused. I'd no useful suggestions to offer, and I very much wanted to hear him out.

"Right . . . So we come to the second point, which is related to the first. For the rest of the gang to feel safe after a transfer, they'd have to be sure that Mrs. Morland wouldn't be able to give any significant information about them—descriptions, names, habits, activities, conversations, clues about the place she'd been shut up in—that might lead us to them afterwards. Could they be sure? She's already been held for well over a week, and it'll be at least another week before any exchange arrangements can be settled. It's almost inconceivable that she won't have learned something about them and their setup in that time. I'm not saying it's impossible—but it isn't easy to imagine the circumstances. If it were merely a matter of collecting a ransom, they could do what many other kidnappers have done—kill the hostage, and pick up the cash. But a transfer is something else. Either they're extraordinarily confident about the conditions they've kept her in or they're hoping in some way to double-cross us on the exchange. This worries me. . . ."

George eased the butt of his cigarette from its holder and stubbed it out in an ashtray with a couple of vicious jabs.

"Finally we come to their third danger—and it's the greatest of all. Presumably they'll try to keep the exchange point a secret until the last moment, in the hope of a clean getaway before we can mobilize forces against them. That might have worked once, but these days there are gadgets. You probably know about them. Miniaturized transmitters that give a bleep and can easily be tracked. We've not yet got to the point where they can be safely swallowed and still function, but we could carry one in whatever transport we used—or in a dozen other places. They're so tiny that they can be concealed in the heel of a shoe, the case of a watch, the butt of a gun—or just stitched into clothing. Wherever our exchange party was directed to, whatever devious route it was instructed to take, it could be pinpointed by cross bearings hour by hour, minute by minute, right up to the rendezvous. By the time the exchange took place, we'd have the whole area sealed off and saturated with men, and they wouldn't have a hope. So what's their plan?"

"Perhaps they're stupid," I said. "Perhaps they haven't heard of the miracles of science."

George shook his head. "I'd like to think so—but I don't believe it. Not if Lacey is anything to go by. He's sinister, but he's certainly not stupid. And he's quite a craftsman. . . . My feeling is that we're up against a gang of skillful young technicians, wholly misguided but highly intelligent and highly imaginative in their planning. . . . I can hardly wait to hear their terms for the exchange."

31

The next two days passed without any significant development. The kidnappers seemed in no hurry to bring the matter to the crunch, and all we could do was wait. There was some comment in the press about the noncommittal statement that had been issued from Downing Street; some speculation about what might be going on behind the scenes. There were rumors of "secret negotiations," of a possible "deal." There were editorials urging the Cabinet

to stand firm on grounds of principle and the ̣
est, and others advocating surrender on grounds ̣
ity. One theory mooted was that Frank Morland w ̣ ̣ ̣ ̣
to raise substantially his original offer of £250,000 to the
kidnappers—perhaps to as much as a million pounds—in
the hope that the gang might yet be bribed to forgo Lacey
for the time being if the payment was high enough. Even
anarchists, it was pointed out, needed funds. Morland himself still had nothing to say to the press. . . .

For me, the waiting time didn't drag. I was now totally
and very cheerfully absorbed in our secret enterprise, to
the exclusion even of meeting old friends. Many of my
waking hours were passed in trying to foresee the various
situations and problems that might arise after an exchange,
and in working out suitable responses to them. For relaxa-
tion, I spent some time on the basics of the game of chess—
the basics in my case being little more than how the pieces
moved and how they should be set up on the board. Since
Lacey was an expert, it was George's contention that I
should at least know the difference between chess and
checkers.

The lull ended on the third day, when another cassette
reached the Yard by post. George phoned me to say it
had arrived, and that he'd be with me shortly, but he didn't
give any details of its content. All he said was that it had
been posted in Leicester, that it ran for seven minutes,
and that the voice was B.B.C.–announcer type—what, in
his disrespectful way, he called bloodless English. He was
having a typed transcript prepared, since that would be
much easier to assimilate and discuss than a long, spoken
message. An hour later, he turned up at the flat with the
document. He sat silent on the settee, smoking one of his
cigarettes, while I read it through. It ran:

The exchange will take place on Friday, September 18th. It will be in two stages.

The first rendezvous will be a roadside quarry on the Moffat–Peebles road in Scotland (A 701). The quarry is 7.3 miles north of Moffat, on the near side of the road as you travel towards Peebles.

Your party will arrive there at 3:30 P.M. precisely, in one vehicle. You will have Tom Lacey with you. You are allowed two guards, including the driver, and they can be armed with one submachine-gun and one hand-gun each. You will be met at the quarry by a single envoy, in another vehicle.

Your party will be required, each in turn, to remove all clothing and footwear, and submit to a rigorous body search. They will then put on clothing and footwear that we shall provide. They will be required to leave in their vehicle all their personal effects of whatever kind. They will also be required to exchange their weapons for similar weapons that we will supply. Each guard will be given one submachine-gun and one automatic pistol, with ammunition. These may be tested on the spot.

Your two guards and Lacey will then be locked in our envoy's vehicle. Our envoy will drive your party to the exchange point. Mrs. Morland will be brought to the exchange point by two armed men.

The exchange will take place in close range of the guns of both sides. Lacey and Mrs. Morland will move off in opposite directions, passing each other, and will continue until they are both out of range. Our guards will then follow Lacey, and your guards will follow Mrs. Morland, and the exchange will have been accomplished.

It will be clear to you that any attempt at a shoot-out by either side might well result in the death of Mrs. Morland or Lacey or both, and would defeat the purpose of the exercise. Our sole object is to recover Lacey, and no shooting will be started from our side.

If there is any attempt to follow our envoy's vehicle from

the quarry, by car or helicopter or in any other way, the operation will not proceed and Mrs. Morland will suffer as already indicated.

If for any reason your party fails to present itself at the exchange point, our side will withdraw and within twelve hours Mrs. Morland will suffer as indicated.

You are to put an advertisement in the personal column of the *Daily Telegraph* during the next two days, giving the chest and leg measurements and shoe sizes of your two guards. The insertion of the advertisement will be taken as your acceptance of our instructions.

32

I laid aside the transcript—as lucid and chillingly arrogant a document as I had ever read—and looked questioningly at George. In the field we had now entered, I was the merest tyro. It was his judgment that mattered.

"Have you digested it?" I asked.

"More or less."

"So—what do you make of it?"

"Well—as we thought, they're not stupid. Very much the reverse. They've obviously foreseen the chief danger we talked about—the gadget—and they've come up with a complete answer. We're going to leave that quarry—assuming we decide to go there—in *their* vehicle, in *their* clothes, and with *their* weapons, having first been stripped as naked as newborn babes. That rules out transmitters—and it means our side won't have a clue about the exchange point until we're actually there and the transfer is taking place. Which maximizes their chance of a clean getaway before the area can be sealed. Grudgingly, I give them full marks for their elaborate plan. There's a very able brain at work."

I said, "Suppose their envoy's vehicle *was* trailed from the quarry—would he know?"

"On that road, almost certainly. I've never been over it myself, but I'm told the A 701 in that part of Scotland is one of the loneliest stretches in the country. It runs for something like twenty miles through bare moorland and climbs to well over a thousand feet with wide visibility—so there'd be no chance whatever of an inconspicuous tail by car. And a helicopter announces itself by its noise. . . . Anyhow, since getting Mrs. Morland away safely would be our first priority, we'd be crazy to take the risk. As I'm sure they realize."

That made sense. I looked again at the transcript, and raised another point. "They talk, rather surprisingly, of sending only one man to the quarry. Why do you think that is?"

"I've been wondering," George said. "I'd have expected two. Of course, it's possible they're short-handed. These terrorist gangs aren't usually large, and a couple of their men will be fully occupied in taking Mrs. Morland to the exchange point. . . . Alternatively, they may be trying to allay any fears we might have about a possible ambush at the quarry—a quick and violent rescue of Lacey, with no exchange."

"Could that happen?"

"They could try it—but I very much doubt if they would. Not with two well-armed guards at the ready. They'd know that Lacey would be the first and instant casualty if shooting started. And, above everything, they want Lacey alive."

"What about the weapons exchange? Might they not hand over some duds?"

George gave a thin smile. "Now there, dear boy, you do me less than justice."

"You'd be there yourself, would you?"

"I'd be there with all guns checked, loaded, and pointed."

"And the other guard?"

"Someone else who knows a barrel from a stock. I've a man in mind, if we get that far."

"How about their plan for the actual exchange? The transfer within gun range. Do you see it as safe for us?"

George shrugged. "Who knows what's safe? It looks all right on paper, but a lot would depend on the terrain, and they have the choice of ground. Obviously we'd have to be extremely watchful. Fingers on triggers. Not giving them the slightest advantage. Ready to take a life for a life. It would be a bit of a gamble, but I think we could handle it."

"You sound very confident, George. Haven't you *any* reservations about their plan?"

"Of course I have," George said. "The obvious one."

"What's that?"

"Would their envoy accept you as Lacey in full daylight?"

"Ah!" Strangely, I hadn't thought about the 3:30 P.M. aspect. I thought about it now.

"Well," I said, "we could only try it and see. My guess is that I would be accepted, even in daylight. For one thing, the envoy would be *expecting* to see Lacey. So he'd be receptive. When he saw me, he'd take it for granted I was Lacey. . . . Apart from that, he'd be preoccupied with all the jobs he had to do. Exchange of clothes, guns. Bodily searches. I should think, too, he'd be under some stress."

95

"Stress?"

"Surely? After all, there'd be nothing to prevent us just taking him in. We'd lose Sally Morland, but we'd have one more of the gang. He'd know that. I can't imagine he'd feel wholly secure."

"It's a point," George conceded.

"Anyway," I said, "it would give us the chance to put the impersonation to the ultimate test—in safety. Better then than later. If he did happen to rumble me, we could just pull out. End of project."

"And they'd kill Mrs. Morland."

"They'll probably do that in any case if they don't get Lacey."

"True."

"On the other hand, if I passed the daylight test, things should get steadily better. . . . By the time the envoy had got through his chores and driven us to the exchange point, evening might well be drawing on. With luck, their plan could be exactly what we discussed earlier—an exchange at dusk, and escape in darkness. For them—*and* for me!"

George grunted, and fell silent.

"So what are you going to recommend?" I asked finally.

"That," he said, "is entirely up to you. . . . I think now there is a distinct possibility that an exchange could go through, and that Sally Morland could be safely recovered. I've no such confidence that you would be safe after the exchange. I've no confidence that you would be able to get away. I think, as I said before, that you're the pawn in the game, the lamb to the slaughter. So it's for you to decide."

I said, "There's a little matter of a quarter of a million pounds, George—remember? *And* there's Sally Morland.

. . . I appreciate your concern for me, but I think we should accept the terms."

"Very well. . . ." George got up. "In that case, I'll report that our feasibility study is finished, and recommend that we go ahead."

He telephoned me shortly after eleven that night. The recommendation, he said, had been approved at top level, and the advertisement, with the required information, would be appearing in the *Telegraph* within twenty-four hours.

33

Something happened next day that I hadn't for a moment foreseen—and it caught me right off balance. John Borley rang up! I'd been so immersed in the exchange plan that I'd almost forgotten I was a professional actor in urgent need of a job—but John hadn't. And that morning—in fact, while I was checking on the *Telegraph* to see if our advertisement was in—he came on the phone with an offer. One of life's little ironies!

"It won't put you in the top tax bracket," he warned, though he sounded quite pleased about it. "Geoffrey Mills, Max Haven's understudy in *Crime for Tea* at the Phoenix, has had a car crash, poor fellow. Nothing desperate, but he's temporarily out of action. So they'd like you to understudy for six weeks minimum, maybe longer. The pay's ninety a week. Not princely, but it's better than a poke in the eye. Money for jam, actually. The part's right up your street—you'll have no problem with it. . . . They'd like you to show at the Phoenix at eleven tomorrow. Okay if I say yes?"

I'd been thinking fast while he talked. Obviously I couldn't turn the offer down without any explanation— there'd be an argument, a row, probably a breach. And I didn't want that. Equally, I couldn't give John an inkling of what I was up to. . . . I could say I didn't fancy being an understudy, reminding him of the old crack about "ruining your reputation in obscurity." But that would come strangely from an unemployed actor who had very little reputation left to lose. . . . I mentally canvassed various ploys, and came up just in time with a disability story based on the misfortune of an acquaintance.

"John," I said, "it's just too bad, but I can't make it. If anything happened to Max, they'd have to carry me on! The fact is, I'm stricken—acute lumbago. Sleeping on a chipboard. Just about able to get to the loo. It's agony. If you've ever had it, you'll sympathize. If not, I do advise against it."

"My dear fellow!" He was all concern. "That is bad news. How did it happen?"

"Well," I said, in a shamefaced voice, "I'm afraid it was entirely my own fault. I got a bit sozzled and fell down in the bathroom. Picked myself up awkwardly—and something gave way. Wham!—just like that. The doc reckons I'll have to use a stick for at least a month."

John tut-tutted. "Bob, you are a bloody fool."

"I know. Perhaps this will be a lesson to me. I really am making an effort now to cut down on the booze. . . . Anyway, thanks for trying, John. Sorry I've let you down. I'll give you a ring when I'm mobile again."

"Do that," John said, without enthusiasm. "Get well quickly." And he rang off.

I mopped my forehead. One day, if I lived, I'd be able to explain. Meanwhile, I didn't think he'd be sending me any grapes.

34

We had less than a week now till D-day, and there were several important jobs still to attend to. One of them was to get my promised issue of clothing from the prison. An emissary from George called to take my measurements, and in a few hours he was back from Berkshire with a comprehensive outfit—a two-piece blue suit, shorts and jersey, striped shirt, gray tie, gray socks, black shoes, and blue raincoat. The quality was poor but the fit wasn't at all bad. In these brand-new and convincingly institutional clothes, I would be able to present myself with confidence to the envoy as a man just released from jail.

A few days later, I was chauffeur-driven to the Sussex "clinic" and my stitches were taken out. The skin bordering my eyes felt a bit tight, but there were no noticeable marks, and the small operation had perfectly achieved the slight upward slant that I'd wanted. The scab on my arm was almost off, and required no attention.

Finally, I made an appointment with Harry the barber for a make-up session in the very early morning of D-day.

George was pretty busy with his own preparations, but he found time toward the end of the week to go over with me some final points that concerned my own safety. First, if the exchange went through and Mrs. Morland was recovered, she would be kept under wraps until I was either free or presumed dead. This would prevent the story breaking prematurely, and possibly adding to my danger. Second, on the morning of D-day Lacey would be transferred to another prison, smuggled quickly into a cell with the knowledge only of one or two selected officers, and lodged there in maximum secrecy until the Morland situation was resolved. If he continued to be kept in Berkshire, George said, the fact would be known to all the staff, and might well be noted by reporters ever watchful for a Government move. The information might then reach the kidnappers while I was still in hazard, with disastrous results. I approved both precautions, and George went off cheerfully to put the final touches to his arrangements. I was now all set for our enterprise, and could hardly wait to get started.

Then, forty-eight hours before the deadline, I had a most unpleasant shock.

35

I had rarely done more than glance at the City pages of newspapers, since I had no money to invest and no special interest in financial affairs. But that Tuesday a name in a paragraph happened to catch my eye. It was quite a short paragraph. I've forgotten the actual wording, but the gist of it was this. A company called the Central & Suburban Property Corporation had gone into voluntary liquidation. Central & Suburban was apparently one of a group of companies that had formerly been headed by Frank Morland—the name that had caught my attention. It had been known for some time, the writer said, that this company was having cash-flow problems. A complication had been that a year or so earlier it had made an unsecured loan of £150,000 to Mr. Morland, at that time its chairman—a sum that it had included in its balance sheet under "Sundry Debtors" and had hopefully treated as a cash asset. There was reason to believe that the company was having difficulty in getting the loan repaid.

That was the start—a cloud scarcely bigger than a man's hand. But by next day the financial journalists had gathered more information. It seemed that the Central & Suburban loan wasn't the only one that Morland had received from his group of companies. The *Record*'s city editor had totted up some figures, and he made the total something like £300,000. The cloud was now threateningly cumulus, and on the Wednesday evening it broke in a deluge of rumor. Morland's bank was said to have called in an overdraft of £160,000. It was believed that the Inland Revenue had a substantial outstanding claim, perhaps for as much as £100,000. There was also a reference to a possible Department of Trade inquiry into the group's affairs. In all the reports there was a notable silence about Morland's personal assets. It was beginning to look, even to an uninitiated person like me, as though the Member for East Suffolk, far from being a multimillionaire in good standing, might have been living very nicely thank you on a mixture of reputation and bluff. In which case, if I survived the Lacey operation, I might well get a large slice of nothing.

I was more than uneasy—I was desperately worried. I had to know the facts behind the rumors, and there was only one place I could get them.

36

It was shortly before eleven in the morning when I rang the ex-directory number that Morland had given me. Early enough, I hoped, to find him still at home—and so it proved. He answered the phone himself. I said, "It's Farran. I have to see you urgently." He hesitated for a moment, then said, in a rather thick voice, "Very well, come along now." I remembered that I wasn't supposed to have open contact with him, but the way things were going that probably didn't matter any more. His address was on the card he had given me, and I took a cab to his flat. It was in a luxury block, only a few hundred yards from the House of Commons.

He came to the door with a glass of whisky in his hand. Judging by his flushed face, it wasn't the first of the day. He didn't attempt to shake hands as he let me in. He led the way into a spacious sitting room, elegantly furnished in a professionally impersonal style. There were some books and papers untidily scattered around, and a drained coffee cup on a table. The room looked more like the pad of a wealthy bachelor than the alternative home of a married couple, for no feminine touch was discernible.

"Do you want a drink?" he asked.

I said, "No, thank you."

"Well—let's sit down, anyway. . . . I can guess why you've come. I suppose you've been reading the newspapers."

"Yes."

"So—what do you want to ask me?"

"The obvious question. If the exchange goes through, and I survive, will you be in a position to honor your contract?"

"No," he said.

"Not even in part?"

"No. Some of the figures the newspapers have printed are a gross distortion, but the fact remains that I'm about to be made bankrupt. The papers themselves are partly responsible. They started the rumor that I might increase my offer to the kidnappers. That naturally scared my creditors, and they began the run that's finished me. Much good it will do them!"

I'd got my answer, and at that point I could well have left. But anger forced more questions out of me. I said, "Could you have raised the money if the kidnappers had accepted your original offer?"

He shrugged. "Probably not."

"Then what was the sense in making it?"

"I had no choice. We politicians have to think of our image. I was supposed to be a millionaire. Everyone expected a big offer. My friends, my colleagues, my supporters, my constituents. So I had to make the gesture. But I never thought there was any chance the offer would be taken up—and I was right."

"It was a gamble?"

"You could call it that. . . . I'd say it was betting on a certainty."

"And the contract with me. . . . Was that a gamble, too?"

"Not really. I never believed for a moment that you would survive to claim the money. It seemed to me a suicidal plan. So the question whether I'd be able to pay you or not was academic. . . . Now you don't have to risk your life. You should thank me."

"What about your wife?"

"I've done everything in my power to save her. No one could have done more."

I got to my feet. "Just one more question. Was it your intention to let me go off to the exchange point without telling me the contract was worthless?"

"I assumed you'd have read the papers," he said. "They made the position clear enough to any ordinary intelligence."

I could happily have bashed him, but for all his insolent bravado he was so clearly a man on the canvas that I somehow refrained. Financially ruined, his brief political career almost certainly at an end, his wife in horrible danger . . . I didn't even use the four-letter word that so obviously applied to him. I just went to the door and let myself out.

37

I walked slowly in the general direction of my flat, hardly aware of the route I was taking or the hooting cars as I crossed blindly against lights. I was seething with anger. I remembered what Morland had said in the Commissioner's office—that he disliked the idea of paying a man to risk his life, that he'd feel guilty if anything happened to me. The bloody hypocrite! And now that he'd been exposed, not a word of regret or contrition. Hardly, even, a passing thought for his wife. An out-and-out, hundred-percent bastard!

I was scarcely less angry with myself. I'd been taken for a sucker. I'd allowed myself to be humiliated. I'd been credulous. Naïve. Greedy, too?

Greedy—yes. It had been a preposterous figure to expect—a quarter of a million pounds. I must have been out of my mind. But I'd been so looking forward to that money. I'd had all sorts of exciting thoughts about how I could use it. I'd even imagined myself as an actor-manager, running a modest repertory company. . . . Up to a point, I'd counted on it. My view had been that I'd either get it or I wouldn't need it because I'd be dead. Now, obviously, I was on a hiding to nothing. It wasn't even as though success in the enterprise would bring me any useful publicity, since my name would have to be kept dark for my own safety. There was nothing in it for me now, nothing at all. Common sense left no doubt about that. Risking your neck for a quarter of a million pounds was one thing. Risking it for free was quite another. Who wanted to be an unpaid mercenary? This, quite definitely, was where I walked out. . . .

Naturally, I was sorry for Sally Morland—as I'd have been sorry for anyone in her position. If it hadn't been for that bastard, she might have been safe and free in a matter of hours. Now her prospects were worse than bleak. Certainly I was sorry for her. . . . But it was an impersonal sympathy. I didn't *know* her. She wasn't a friend of mine. And even that generalized sympathy had become a bit blunted. What could a woman be like who could tolerate an arrogant crook like Morland as a husband? For all I knew, she was in on the crookery with him. . . . Anyway, she was the Government's responsibility, not mine. They could save her at any time by letting Lacey go. They could dispatch the real Lacey with George tomorrow. . . . But *would* they? And if they didn't? That smoth-

ered scream on the cassette still haunted me. It wouldn't
be all that easy living with myself afterward. After they'd
found the body . . .

George would understand, of course. George was a real-
ist. He'd understand why I'd had to pack it in. He wouldn't
expect anything else. . . . At least, I hoped he wouldn't.
. . . Telling George wasn't going to be very pleasant. Over
the weeks, I'd come to value his good opinion. And he
was a man who'd have a gimlet eye for anyone chickening
out. Not that he'd ever say that—not that it was true . . .
Hadn't I every right to withdraw? To withdraw with self-
respect and dignity, when I'd been let down by a crook?

Packing it in would leave a gap, of course. In my life
. . . To be honest, a yawning bloody gap. I'd been living
with this project day and night for weeks. I'd thought of
nothing else. And, oddly, I'd been a happy man. Now it
would be back to agent John Borley—and, perhaps, the
bottle. . . . Oh, hell!

I was still mulling things over as I reached the flat.

38

I had barely opened the door when the telephone began
to ring. I went quickly to the sitting room and grabbed
the receiver. It was George on the line.

"I've been trying to get you for the past hour," he said.
His voice had a note of urgency that I could well
understand.

"I've been seeing Morland," I told him.

"Ah! All right, I'm coming round."

I sat down by the telephone, and went over all the arguments again in my mind.

George arrived at one o'clock. It was now less than twenty hours to the deadline we'd fixed for departure. His face was grim.

"Well?" he asked.

"He's bust," I said. "There'll be no money."

He nodded. "That's what it looked like." There was an awkward pause. "I suppose there's an outside chance," he said, "that the Government might fork out something. I've been working on it. But there's not a hope of a decision before tomorrow. The P.M.'s in Paris, lunching with the French President, and he's flying on to Bonn for dinner. Anyway, it's unlikely he'd be prepared to pledge a large slice of public money without consulting his senior colleagues. . . . So there it is. No guarantees . . . Now what do you want me to do? Call off the troops?"

"No," I said.

"It would be the sensible thing."

I shook my head. "Look, George, let's not make a production out of this. No heroics, for Christ's sake . . . But we've gone too far to turn back now. Both of us. All the work we've done, all the planning, all the effort. Damn it, I've even been mutilated in the cause! Now we're all set—and, in the words of that tatty old cliché, the show must go on." I hesitated. "There's something else—a line in a poem. . . . Am I sounding theatrical?"

"A little," George said, "but you've every right to be."

"John Milton—on his blindness. 'And that one talent which is death to hide, lodged with me useless.' I *have* a modest talent, and such as it is I want to use it. To make something of it. I've got the lead part in a great real-life melodrama—perhaps the fattest role I'll ever play—and

I'm bloody well not going to walk out on it on opening night. So what I say is—forget Morland, forget the money—and up with the curtain."

He looked at me doubtfully. "A fine speech! But are you *sure*, dear boy?"

"I'm absolutely sure. I've looked at it all ways, and I've never been more certain of anything in my life."

"All right," George said. "It's your decision. . . . Let's hope you have a long run!"

PART TWO

THE ACTION

I was up at crack of dawn on the morning of D-day. The indoor thermometer showed eighty-three degrees and the cloudless sky threatened yet another scorcher. I made some coffee, showered and shaved, and dressed in my prison issue, wishing the jacket and trousers were of lighter weight. Then I called a radio cab and drove to Chelsea, where Harry the barber was waiting to do his stuff. By seven-thirty my beard, mustache, and wig were securely attached to me, my eyebrows were suitably tinted, and the parts of my face uncovered by hair were very slightly touched up to make me even more like Lacey's photograph. The refinements wouldn't last, but they might help to get me through the crucial daylight encounter.

George picked me up at the studio at eight o'clock. He was wearing a tan safari-type outfit, just the job for a day on the moors, and he looked enviably cool. There was a bulge in a side pocket, which I thought was probably a handgun. He inspected me closely, removed a blond hair from my jacket, approved my general appearance, checked that I had absolutely nothing on my person except clothes, and led the way downstairs.

The waiting car was a 3½-liter Jaguar, fast and comfortably spacious. Its interior was protected from glare by tinted glass, see-through from the inside but a dark screen against prying eyes from outside. The driver's door was open, and a man was sitting at the wheel in his shirt sleeves. George said, "Sergeant Shafto—Mr. Farran," and we gripped hands. Shafto was a big, solid, reliable-looking man with a friendly grin. On the seat beside him was a rug, not quite concealing the barrels of two submachine guns.

I got into the back with George, shedding my jacket for comfort, and we set off.

As we left the curb, another car—a large blue one parked fifty yards away—fell into line behind us. I watched it as it tailed us round a couple of corners, then looked at George with concern. "Someone seems to be following us."

"Our backup car to Moffat," he said. "Just in case of breakdown. This is one appointment we can't afford to miss."

George thought of everything. At least, that's how it seemed to me then.

2

It was a long drive to Moffat—almost three hundred and fifty miles, according to the A.A. book. Nobody was very chatty. At this stage there was nothing of importance to discuss, and the uncertainties ahead were too much on our minds for light conversation. From time to time, George and Shafto swapped places to share the driving load. There were sandwiches and coffee in the car, and we lunched briefly in a lay-by. Afterward I dozed a little. Not surprisingly, with action imminent and an alarm clock set for dawn, I'd had an almost sleepless night. But I was still too keyed up to get much rest.

We plugged on up the motorway at a steady seventy, seeing little but other traffic and the yellow desert that the summer had made of the surrounding fields, and feeling very thankful for our tinted glass. Somewhere around the border the motorway ended for us, but after we left it we were still on a fast double carriageway, and we were well up to schedule.

A few miles short of Moffat, with the tension rising, George gave me some final words of caution and advice.

"Remember," he said, "that from the moment we reach the quarry, you are on one side, Shafto and I are on the other. You're Lacey the gunman; we're the law. The vehicle they bring may be wired for sound—so no fraternizing, no cooperation, even when we're alone. You hate our guts, we hate yours. Much of the time there'll be a loaded pistol at your back. Don't appear indifferent to it. Lacey wouldn't."

"I'll remember."

"Now another thing. You've been brought here as my prisoner—and a dangerous one. In normal circumstances, if you were Lacey I'd have you handcuffed to me. As it is, I'll need my hands free for my gun. The envoy will understand that. But *you* must be in handcuffs, at least to start with—just to give the right impression."

I nodded. George reached to the shelf behind him. I held out my hands, and he snapped the cuffs on my wrists.

"Last thing of all—a small present for you." He gave me a tiny box, which I opened. There was a phial inside, thumbnail size. "Cyanide," he said. "You just crunch it up in your teeth. I doubt if it's as painless as they say, but I can vouch for its speed. . . . If the moment comes, dear boy, don't leave it too late."

I slipped the phial into my trousers pocket. I tried to

think of some crack to relieve the strained silence in the car, but couldn't. The planning and the theorizing were over, and this was the moment of truth. What had started as an intriguing thought, a stimulating idea, had suddenly become a frightening reality.

3

We stopped briefly just beyond Moffat. The blue car, still close on our tail, pulled up a hundred yards behind us. The Jag's clock showed 3:15 P.M., so we had a few minutes in hand. "No point in getting there before time," George said. "Always a sign of weakness." The sun was blazing from a brassy sky, and we were all sweating. My mouth was dry, and not just from the heat. We drank some tea from a flask. George said to Shafto, "If it's possible, Mike, park us in the quarry between their vehicle and the sun." Shafto took the point and said, "Okay." When we moved off again, George had one of the Sten guns across his knees.

We climbed steadily. We were out now in open moorland, a parched expanse of undulating slopes, blackened here and there by summer fires that had consumed everything above the soil. As we climbed, the scenery grew wilder and grander. For miles at a stretch, there were no houses or farms, no buildings of any sort. Except for a few sheep that moved reluctantly off the road as we approached, and one lorry that came from the opposite direction, there were no signs of life anywhere. To our left, empty hills; to our right, the virgin water of the infant

Tweed, with not even an angler in sight. Presently, on a short straight stretch, the blue car shot past us and went on its way with a toot of farewell. Shafto was watching his odometer. "Almost there," he said, and slowed. We rounded a bend, and saw the entrance to the quarry on our left. George wound his window right down and poked the tip of his gun out. We nosed cautiously in. It was a large quarry, long ago worked out and abandoned, with a flat spacious floor partly hidden from the road by a clump of stunted bushes. A black van, about the size of a Dormobile, was parked well inside. Shafto maneuvered the Jaguar so that the sun was behind us, and cut the engine. I braced myself for the test of a lifetime.

A man emerged from the driving seat of the van. He was a youngish, slim man. Hollow-cheeked, almost gaunt. He was wearing a deerstalker hat with the peak pulled well down over his forehead, oversize dark glasses, and a light, colored scarf swathed around his chin. Otherwise his dress was a T-shirt and jeans. The combination was bizarre, but it gave him effective concealment. Not quite as effective as a stocking mask, but much less likely to start a rumpus if some other motorist should happen to turn in to the quarry.

He strolled toward us, the sun in his eyes. He was unarmed. Shafto and George opened their near-side doors. The envoy came up to the car and looked in. Looked at me.

"Hi, Chris," he said.

So I wasn't Tom—I was Chris! At least to him. "Hi," I said. "Good to see you."

"Who's in charge?" he asked.

"I am," George said.

The envoy noticed my handcuffs. "You've got a gun,"

he said to George. "There's no need for those things. Take them off."

George appeared to hesitate, then shrugged. "He's more likely to get a bullet without them. Just one careless move, and I'll shoot. . . . Still, it's his funeral." He unlocked the cuffs and freed my wrists. "So—what's the drill?"

"One at a time into the van. You come first and bring your weapons."

George motioned to Shafto. Shafto got out of the driving seat and took over the job of guarding me. George followed the envoy to the van and climbed into the back of it. From where we were we couldn't see inside, and it was too far away for us to hear anything that was said.

Shafto gazed out over the moors and river below us, and up to the lip of the quarry, ready to open up at the first sign of a hostile move. But nothing stirred except sheep. "Okay so far," he murmured. "Nice work—Chris!"

In a few minutes, George reappeared. He was dressed now in a set of blue denim overalls. He had a submachine gun in one hand and an automatic in the other. Outside the van, he took the machine gun apart and reassembled it with practiced ease as the envoy looked on. Presently he pointed it skyward, and fired a short burst and a single shot. Then he examined the automatic and fired a shot from that. He looked toward Shafto and raised a thumb.

"You next," the envoy called to Shafto. The "you" sounded like "yeou." No bloodless English from him. South London, I thought. Ugly whining vowels . . .

George stationed himself by the car and took over guard duty. Not for a second was I to be left uncovered by one or the other. Shafto disappeared into the van, and the procedure was repeated. He emerged in similar blue denims, and checked his new weapons with equal efficiency.

The envoy called, "Your turn, Chris. Come on over." I got out of the car and walked toward him, closely imitating Lacey's light-footed gait. George followed a couple of feet behind me with the Sten. Shafto was watching the moor again, ceaselessly vigilant.

The envoy said, "What's that gear you're wearing, Chris?"

"Prison issue for the parting guest," I told him.

"Shoes, too?"

"Yes. The whole outfit."

He nodded. "Just as well I came prepared. Those things could be fixed. . . . Step into the parlor, will you?"

I climbed into the van, and he followed me. It was darkish inside; it must have been even darker for him, with his sunglasses. So far, Lady Luck was with me. . . . George watched us from the outside, still covering me.

The envoy produced jeans, a T-shirt, a light denim jacket, and a pair of well-worn shoes. "Your old friends," he said, indicating the shoes. I said "Ah!" as though I recognized them. I stripped to my underpants, and put the clothes on. There was no body search for me—I was trusted. I felt in the pocket of my prison trousers and took out a prison handkerchief with George's phial concealed in it, and transferred it to a denim pocket. A dicey moment—but it passed without mishap. Finally I put on Lacey's shoes. They were the wrong size for me, and they pinched badly. This was a development that no one had thought of—not even George. . . . Though even if he had, I couldn't see there was much he could have done about it. Anyway, I was stuck with the things now. I could hardly say they didn't fit!

We climbed down. The envoy glanced around the quarry. "Right, that's it. We're ready to leave."

"What about the guns we brought?" George asked.

"I'll keep them. A fair exchange . . . We'll lock everything else up in your car."

He gathered up our discarded clothes and shoes, and himself took them to the Jag. I guessed he was making sure that no one picked up a transmitter from the car at the last moment. He put the clothes on the back seat, with the pair of handcuffs on top, and covered everything with a rug. Then he locked the car and brought the key to George.

"Okay," he said, "into the van, all of you." His hand fell lightly on my shoulder. "Not too long now, Chris!" I gave his arm a friendly slap, American style, and we piled in.

There were no seats—just a hard metal floor and some bits of old sacking, on which we disposed ourselves as best we could. The envoy pulled a rear shutter down, and we heard a click as he locked it. There was a shutter across the front, too, cutting us off from the driving cab. If it hadn't been for a gleam of light from a ventilator, we'd have been in total darkness, for there were no windows. It was going to be an uncomfortable ride.

4

There was a clatter from the front of the van—our guns, I thought, being stowed on the floor—and the off-side door slammed. After that, there was total silence for perhaps a minute. The envoy making sure there was no helicopter around? Then the engine came noisily to life, and we set off, bumping over the uneven quarry floor, slowing at the exit, and turning so imperceptibly in to the road that from our dark cage it was almost impossible to know whether we'd swung left or right. What soon became apparent was that we were going downhill. But which way? Back, down to Moffat? Or on, down toward Peebles? Who could tell?

I eased myself out of Lacey's shoes. It wasn't so much that they were the wrong size; they were entirely the wrong shape. Lacey, evidently, had a narrow instep and a long foot. I had a broad instep and a short foot. So my toes were tightly compressed and there was a chafing looseness at the heel. My old friends, indeed!

I sat back and tried to relax. After all, we hadn't done too badly so far. The first encounter had gone off without a hitch. There'd been no ambush, no shooting, no trouble. Both sides had stuck meticulously to the agreed terms, which promised well for the exchange. And my own worst hurdle was now behind me. With a little help from the sun and the envoy's dark glasses and Harry the barber's expertise and some convincing play with the handcuffs, I'd passed the daylight test. And if I could get by in bright daylight, why shouldn't I get by altogether? I wasn't exactly bubbling over with confidence, but I was less apprehensive than I had been on the way up to Moffat.

The heat in the van was fierce, and I soon shed my denim jacket. The sun, an enemy all the summer, beat mercilessly on the panels. Fortunately there were some tiny cracks in the front shutter, not wide enough to see through, but giving us a welcome draft. It was so dark that I could barely make out George and Shafto, backed against the off-side wall of the van. From time to time, they muttered to each other. They didn't speak to me and, obeying instructions, I didn't speak to them.

It was, of course, quite impossible to know what route we were taking. Sometimes the road was uphill, sometimes steeply downhill. Sometimes we traveled slowly as though in a narrow lane; sometimes fast as though on a safe double track. George tried once to peer out of the ventilator, but from his negative grunt I concluded there was no clear view through it. One could only guess at the passage of time, for none of us had a watch. George and Shafto had had to leave theirs behind in the Jaguar, with all the rest of their effects.

Occasionally there were identifiable sounds above the engine noise: the sharp rattle of flints from a newly sprayed surface, the rumble of heavy traffic alongside us, a distant police siren, a blast of music from a radio, voices when we stopped—presumably at traffic lights in some town we were passing through. Then on again at speed. Or was it back again? We couldn't know. We might be making a long journey. Or we might be going round and round in a deliberately misleading circle. One thing was certain—when we arrived at our destination, we wouldn't have the slightest idea where we were.

In the end, the trip became rugged. We were flung about, with little to hold on to, as the van bumped and lurched in low gear over broken ground. We could have been on a field track—we were certainly no longer on a made-up road. The going became steadily rougher. There was nothing audible now except the creak and rattle of the van's own movement and the noise of the straining engine. We continued, perhaps for fifteen minutes, to bounce and bang our way uphill. Then—blessed relief!—the van stopped. The engine cut, and for a few moments there was dead silence. Then there was movement in the driver's cab, and we heard the envoy climb out and walk round to the back. A key scraped, and the shutter went up. It was still daylight outside—dazzling to our eyes after the darkness. The air that wafted in was sweetly scented but oppressively hot. No respite yet from the furnace! All the same, the day's sun was losing its power. At a guess, there was little more than an hour till dusk.

The envoy said, "Okay—you can come out." I forced my feet back into Lacey's shoes, picked up my jacket, and went down first, with George's gun in my back. Shafto followed. And we all looked around.

We were still in wild country. Beautiful country. Totally empty country. As empty as the moors near Moffat, but subtly different. On either side of us there were smooth steep slopes, cut into patterns by low dry-stone walls. Ahead of us the ground rose up a narrowing valley, perhaps by a thousand feet, to a short, flat horizon, bounded by crags and sharply etched against the sinking sun.

The envoy pointed up the valley. "The exchange will take place at the top," he said. "All you have to do is keep going." He raised a farewell hand to me. "We'll be seeing you, Chris."

I nodded, and raised a hand in response.

He still had his camouflage of deerstalker and scarf and huge glasses. Not one of us could have given a useful description of him.

5

We turned away, and set off slowly toward the far horizon. It was good to be out of the van, but no one was feeling exactly sprightly. We had been, at a rough estimate, two and a half hours in the hot box, and the joggling of the last stretch had almost emulsified us. My cramped feet were painful, the left one worse than the right, and I had to limp to keep going.

Shafto led the way and I followed close behind him. George brought up the rear, his automatic a foot from my back. No one watching us from the heights could have supposed that I was anything but a prisoner. Both men had their Stens slung handily for instant action, and both were closely scrutinizing the surrounding hills for any sign of trouble.

Behind us, we heard the van reverse and roar away along the downhill track. The envoy, presumably, had other business to attend to. For the first time in hours, we could safely talk.

I gazed around at the empty slopes. "Do you have any thoughts about where we might be, George?"

"Not a clue, dear boy. I never was strong on local topography. . . . It could still be Scotland, I suppose—or the Lakes, or Yorkshire—or even North Wales at a pinch. . . . Good sporting country, anyway!"

"Good holiday country, too," I said. "Just the job for hikers. I'm surprised there's no one around."

"Our friends have chosen a good time. Well on into September, a weekday, and dusk approaching. Rough ground, tricky in the dark. So a fair bet they wouldn't be interrupted."

Shafto half turned. "At this stage," he said, "they'd probably knock off any stranger who got in their way. What have they got to lose?"

There was only one answer to that. Nothing.

We trudged slowly up the narrowing valley. There wasn't any path or track to follow, only a general upward direction. The way was strewn with sharp rocks and precariously balanced boulders, hard on the ankles in the fading light. To the left there was a steep grassy slope, with patches of dried-up heather and brown bracken and gray granite outcrops. To the right there was another slope, broken by precipitous spurs of crag. Nothing moved except sheep, sneezing their startled alarm as we disturbed them. We kept to the center of the valley, plodding upward beside a peaty stream, a mere trickle that in wet weather would no doubt have been a torrent. Once we stopped and drank from it, and the brown water was like nectar to our parched lips. Our goal was farther away than it had looked—a good two miles from the start, I reckoned— and the last pitch was going to be steep scree. By now, Lacey's shoes were giving me hell at every step. I tried not to think about it, to make light of it. What, after all, were a few blisters, when you were carrying a phial of cyanide in your pocket? Philosophy didn't help. I had a toenail pressing into flesh, and a chafed heel, and they hurt.

We took the last quarter of a mile at a near crawl. The angle to the ridge was about seventy-five degrees. One step forward up the loose stones was followed by half a step back in a slither of rubble. I was breathing hard from the climb—or was it, as the moment approached, from fear? Sweat poured like water down my arms and body. There was a stickiness now in my left shoe. An ooze of blood . . .

We were nearing the top. The light was going. This at least was something we'd been right about—the exchange at dusk.

George said, "We're almost there, dear boy. How are you feeling?"

"A touch of first-night nerves, George . . . It'll probably pass when I'm on stage."

He gave me a gentle poke in the back with his gun. "That's in lieu of a handshake . . . The very best of luck, Bob! We'll be waiting to hear from you." And Shafto echoed the "Good luck!"

We breasted the final slope and were out on a grassy plateau. The view in the dying light was majestic. We stood on a watershed. On either side there were towering granite cliffs, black against the pale sky. Behind us was the long valley we'd climbed. Before us, the ground dropped away, even more steeply. Far in the distance, lights were beginning to twinkle. Just ahead of us there were figures.

6

We moved with infinite care to the confrontation. Shafto, his submachine gun at the ready, stepped a little to one side to reduce our target surface. George had pocketed his handgun and was covering me with the barrel of his Sten. Their well-rehearsed actions had the precision of a ballet. In the half-light I could now make out a party of three, approaching us with equal caution. Two of them were men, armed with submachine guns and wearing stocking masks. The third was slighter but shapely—unmistakably a woman. There was a gun barrel at her back, too.

We advanced till we were within speaking distance of the group. Then George said sharply, "Hold it, Lacey!" and I stopped. Ten yards separated us from the enemy. There was a moment of tense silence, ended by one of the men. "Come forward, Chris," he said. "Go forward, Mrs. Morland. Move slowly, both of you. We don't want any accidents."

George gave me a light prod. I stepped ahead. So did Sally Morland. We passed each other with scarcely a glance. Two Sten guns were trained on her, and two on me. If anyone lost his cool now, there'd be a bloodbath.

George moved toward Sally. One of the men approached me. He looked closely at me through his stocking mask in the dwindling light. "Welcome back, Chris."

"Jesus," I said, "that was some climb!"

I glanced back. George was talking quietly to Mrs. Morland, but his eyes were on the enemy. Shafto still had me covered.

"That's all," the man called to George. "You can take her away."

George turned and set off back down the valley with the girl. The man grasped my arm, and we also took a few steps—down the opposite valley. For a few moments the two rear guards remained silhouetted on the col, covering the dual retreat. Then Shafto's head disappeared below the horizon, and the other man joined us.

It was over! The rescue plan had worked, and worked perfectly. The phony exchange had gone through without a hitch. Sally Morland was safe and free. Tom Lacey was still in jail, and would remain there. A brilliant coup, brilliantly executed . . .

It should have been a moment of triumph, but I was far from feeling triumphant. I just felt very much alone.

7

The two men peeled off their stocking masks as we set off down the valley. In the dim light, I could make nothing of their features. One of them was short and stocky, the other tall and slim. Both were wearing jeans, T-shirts, and casual jackets, similar to the clothes I'd been given by the envoy. Both now had their guns slung across their chests.

We dropped down for a couple of hundred feet or so. Then the tall man said, "Hang on a moment," and we all stopped. He was looking back toward the plateau and listening. In the still evening air a dislodged pebble would have been audible, but the only sounds were a bird twittering and sheep munching. "All clear," he said, "no one's following us," and we started off again.

The two set a hot pace among the rocks and boulders, and I lagged. Not deliberately to hold them up—I was incapable of going faster. The tall one, who seemed to be in charge, said "We've got to get a move on, Chris." His accent was what used to be called "public school," and I guessed he was the one who'd dictated the exchange terms on the last cassette. "You're limping, aren't you," he said. "Something wrong with your foot?"

I couldn't deny it—it was obvious. And I didn't dare blame the shoes. A couple of miles uphill in "old friends" would hardly have left me in this state. But I had to give some explanation. I said, "There was a bit of a punch-up in the prison. Day before yesterday. I got floored, and twisted an ankle. Nothing serious—just painful."

The tall one said to the other, "We'd better give him a hand, Jim." I made a mental note that the stocky one was "Jim." It was time I began to call them by their first names. They gave me an arm, one on each side. Their support did little to ease the pain in my foot, but it left me no choice about moving faster. Their pace was now mine.

Jim said, "We should be okay for time, Rex." He was

American—or his accent was. Boston, rather than Brooklyn. A flavor of the campus . . . "How long would you say before they get to a phone?"

"An hour, at least," Rex said.

"How about if one of them shoved on ahead?"

"It would still take an hour. Eddie worked it out that it would be four miles from the col to the first house— and rough going all the way, even on the track. We can trust Eddie—you know how good he is with maps."

Eddie? Perhaps the envoy . . .

"Sure," Jim said. "That's okay, then. In an hour we'll have faded."

They sounded confident. All the same, the pace quickened—and there were moments when I could have shouted with pain. The descent was steep, much steeper than the other valley had been, and in the gathering darkness it was impossible to be sure of a firm foothold. There were more patches of loose scree, and several times we all slid down together in a chaos of legs and arms and guns. I was in such trouble that I began to wonder if I'd make it to the bottom. Then, quite suddenly, the ground leveled out and we were on smooth turf, and there was a plantation of conifers standing out sharply against the western sky. Jim said, "There's our jalopy," and pointed. I saw with relief that there was a car parked at the edge of the trees. Beyond it I could just make out the vague outline of a track leading on down the valley. Now I could understand the assurance of the two men. For them, it had been a quick, short hike from the exchange point to their transport. Whereas George and Shafto and Sally must still be miles from a phone.

We stayed by the car for a couple of minutes, drinking tepid but welcome Coke from cans that Rex produced.

The plantation behind me was black and inviting. This should have been my moment to make a dash for freedom. Once I was away among the trees, I could probably have lost them. But in the state I was in, it was hopeless. A sentence came wryly to mind—"My feet are killing me." It could be literally true, but there was nothing I could do about it.

We slung the Coke cans into the undergrowth and piled into the car. Jim took the wheel. Rex got in beside him, cradling one of the Stens with the barrel pointing outward. I slumped down on the back seat and eased Lacey's Iron Maidens from my bruised and lacerated toes.

It was quite dark now, and I could see little of the route we were taking. The vestigial track continued downhill for perhaps a mile before broadening into a lane, which soon became a minor road and then a major one. The atmosphere in the car was tense, and the talk was staccato. Much of it was about the route, in which I could take no part. Jim was driving fast, racing to beat any cordon that might be thrown. I was in two minds about whether I'd have welcomed a police check. When you're with gangsters, you tend to share their fate. If we ran into a roadblock, I hadn't the least doubt that Rex would start shooting. So, presumably, would the police. I might survive, or I might not. . . .

From time to time, as we slowed through built-up areas—"Keep your head down, Chris"—I glimpsed a name sign in the car's lights. A town's coat of arms, with attractions pictorially displayed. "Careful motorists welcomed!" Windermere. Kendal. So the exchange point had been in the Lake District, somewhere up in the high fells. I said, "Where exactly were we, Rex? Where was the switchover?" He turned in his seat. "Between Pasture Beck and Kentmere. You wouldn't know them. Eddie worked it out. He'll show you later on the map."

I said, "He chose a good spot. Stroke of genius." As, indeed, it had been.

After Kendal, I lost all sense of direction and place. The road was now a winding one, with few villages and no towns. The country became hilly again, with steep gradients. Jim muttered as he worked at his gears. "We grabbed a lousy auto this time, Rex. No power at all." But the sense of urgency had gone from the car. The panel clock showed almost nine o'clock. We must have covered something like fifty miles since the exchange. So there could no longer be any danger—or hope—of a cordon. No one could cordon off a complex network of roads with a diameter of a hundred miles. We were out in the open, as free from inspection as any other car.

Suddenly Jim slowed. He seemed to be looking out for a turning. Then he swung left, into a lane that was only just wide enough to hold us. We were climbing all the time now, mostly in first gear. Climbing and winding, between more dry-stone walls. The lane surface deteriorated. The going became very rough. Once more we were on some sort of track. And once more we were getting into high moorland country. Soon there wasn't even a track. A sliver of moon had risen in the east, illuminating the contours of wild hills. Jim doused his lights and we crept cautiously forward, still climbing. Then the ground flattened, and we pulled up.

"Well, we've made it!" Rex said. "Nice driving, Jim! And full marks for Eddie when we see him." He got out of the car, taking the guns with him. Somehow I managed to get Lacey's shoes back on. I got out, too, and gazed around.

Except for the moonlit moorscape, and what looked like

a circle of low bushes right ahead, there was absolutely nothing to be seen. I hadn't the slightest idea where we were, or why. I took a tentative step, testing my feet after their rest in the car, and again wrote off any hope of immediate escape. For the moment I was virtually a cripple. I'd be overtaken before I'd gone twenty yards. . . .

Rex was pointing to the circle of bushes. "The Devil's Cauldron," he said, improbably. As I stared at him in bewilderment, he added, "That's what the map calls it. Come and take a look. Careful, though . . ." I limped with him to the bushes. Underfoot, everything was bare rock—the fleshless bones of the earth. At a gap in the bushes he held me back. I looked down, and saw that I was standing on the rim of a gaping hole. It was unfenced, perhaps fifty feet across, and awesome.

"It's about ninety feet deep," Rex said. "We plumbed it. There's water at the bottom, but you can't see it from here, even in daylight. Twenty feet of water, we think. If there's an outlet, it must have got blocked. And at that depth there's not much evaporation—even in a drought. . . . It's our dustbin."

What happened next was almost beyond belief. Rex drew me to one side. Jim drove the car very slowly to the edge of the hole, cut the engine, and got out. He walked to the rear of the car and gave the chassis a heave and a push. It must have been standing on a slightly downhill slope. Inch by inch, it began to move. Gradually it gathered momentum. It reached the lip of the hole, dipped at the edge—and went in. There were long seconds of silence. Then a hollow reverberation came up from the depths, and silence fell again.

"Right," Rex said. "Refuse disposed of . . . Now—home, James, eh?"

8

He took my arm again, the considerate comrade, and helped me along, while Jim walked beside us with the guns. I couldn't imagine what or where we were making for in such a wilderness. If it was far, they'd soon have to carry me. Footwise, I was near my limit. By comparison, the sticky heat was only a secondary discomfort. Though these moors, judging by our long climb in the car, could well be a couple of thousand feet above sea level, the motionless air was as oppressive as it had been in the valleys.

One thing only was clear to me. Whatever we were doing, and wherever we were going, I wasn't expected to have previous knowledge of it. Otherwise Rex wouldn't have told me in near-guidebook terms about the Cauldron. I was the old pal just out of prison, being shown around some place, some setup, I was unfamiliar with. So I could be surprised, gratified, critical, anything but informed—without danger. It was useful to know.

Leaning heavily on Rex, I stumbled forward over moonlit rock and dried-up turf for perhaps a hundred yards. Then, in a shallow, saucer-shaped depression, we stopped. "Welcome to our base," Rex said, extending an arm as though he were inviting me to admire some luxurious home. There was nothing to be seen, not even a bush. Just bare ground, stone outcrops, a lunar landscape. I gazed hard into his face, suddenly wondering if I'd fallen into the hands of madmen rather than anarchists.

I was wrong to doubt him. He was sane enough—at

least as far as the existence of a "base" was concerned. Jim took a torch from his pocket and flashed it downward. I saw then that there was another hole in the ground, a small one, about four feet in diameter. Rex produced a second torch. He knelt, and fumbled inside the hole, and came up with a rope in his hand, looped at the end. He pulled gently on the rope, and the top of a ladder appeared. It had a dull metallic look about it, and from its obvious lightness I guessed the metal was aluminum. Rex gripped the top rung and shifted the ladder around a little, till it stood firm on whatever was below.

"You go first, Jim," he said. "You can light the way for Chris."

"Okay." Jim handed his guns to Rex, got down on his knees, and lowered himself backward onto the ladder and into the hole. One moment he was there, the next he had vanished.

Rex said, "You next, Chris. There's nothing to worry about. This bit isn't deep."

I looked down. I could see Jim at the bottom, shining his torch. The hole was slightly out of plumb, and had jagged yellowish-white sides. It was far from inviting, but I clearly had no choice. Anyway, by now I was more than curious. I backed into it as Jim had done, felt with my feet for the ladder, grasped the top rung, and cautiously lowered myself. It wasn't far to the bottom—no more than ten or twelve feet. Rex followed me down, slipping the loop of rope over a hook a few inches below the lip of the hole as he passed, and finally drawing the ladder away so that its top would be invisible from the surface.

The hole opened out at the bottom, into a horizontal tunnel. Rex now took the lead, shining his torch on the ground just ahead of me. For a few yards we had to crouch. Then the roof rose, giving us headroom. After a couple of S-bends the passage suddenly widened. Rex halted, an arm outstretched to keep me back. We seemed to be on a kind of platform. Ahead there was nothing but impenetrable darkness. To the right the torches showed an alcove in the rock, with a floor of yellow sand. On the sand there was an inflated air bed with an electric hand lamp beside it.

By now I was prepared for almost anything—but not for what actually happened. Jim, groping in some rocky interstice, found a switch—and lights came on, around us and below.

"Current from a car battery," Rex said. "Jim fixed the wires. We only use it for coming and going, to save the juice. . . . Now you can see why I stopped you."

I looked ahead and down. We were standing on the edge of a precipice. From its lip, another aluminum ladder descended to the floor of a large cave. One corner of the cave was illuminated. It glowed with an amber luster like scenery in a fairy pantomime. One almost expected to hear an orchestra strike up.

There was a wicker basket standing near the lip, with a heavy rope attached to it. Rex put his guns in the basket and lowered it to the cave floor. Jim backed onto the ladder and disappeared into the depths. When he reached the bottom, he called up, "All clear below!"

Rex said, "Your turn, Chris."

I looked with some misgiving at the ladder. I saw that it was hooked at the top over something that had been hammered into a fissure of rock. A piton—was that the word? Something, anyway, that appeared to be an iron spike with a ring at the top. I'd seen similar things being used in climbing films.

Rex said, "It looks worse than it is. The ladder's secured at the bottom. It's quite safe if you hang on tight and don't panic. You'll soon get used to it."

I doubted that. I'd never had much of a head for heights. However, as Lacey I was supposed to be a man of action with an iron nerve. Lacey, I felt sure, would not have hesitated—so I mustn't. I lowered myself onto the ladder and went slowly down. At a guess, the drop from the platform was about forty feet. The lip of the precipice overhung by several feet the inward-slanting wall of rock that stretched away below it, so there was nothing to hold on to on the way down except the ladder itself—a sectional affair that at moments swayed alarmingly in space. Still, I made it safely to the cave floor. The bottom of the ladder, I saw, was jammed against a lump of rock to prevent it shifting.

Rex followed me down, descending fast with the confidence of practice.

From where I now stood, the illuminated part of the cavern was a fantastic sight. There were bunches of stalactites that hung from the roof like some petrified waterfall. There were cascades of snow-white rock, worn to a polished smoothness and marvelously fluted. There were wrinkled curtains of rock that looked as though they could be stirred by a breath of air. There were pedestals and obelisks and organ pipes, wonderfully sculpted and infinitely varied. There were coral flowers, glistening and sparkling in rock niches. I'd been in one or two commercially exploited caves as a tourist, but this beat them all for sheer breath-taking beauty. . . . Not that I was exactly dwelling on beauty at that moment. An enchanted kingdom was all very well, but where was the man with the magic wand to get me out?

I gazed around, taking in all that was visible. In one corner of the cavern, a stream of water gushed from a rift high up in the wall, breaking in spray on the floor and filling the air around it with a fine mist. Then, along one side of the cave, it ran away very gently over clay and pebble dams, leaving motionless pools behind that reflected the distant bulbs of light.

It felt cool below ground—even a little chilly after the humid heat above—and for the first time I was glad of my loose jacket. But the air was dry and fresh, and the change to fifty degrees or thereabouts after the eighty degrees of the surface was a welcome physical relief. I might still sweat down there, but it wouldn't be because of the temperature. . . .

We crossed the floor of the cave, with spikes of young stalagmites snapping and crackling under our feet. Rex lit a Tilley lamp—just one, I noticed, though there were several standing in a row—and switched off the battery lights. Jim had evidently done an expert two-way job with his wiring. There was now a pool of light, illuminating adequately if not brilliantly an area about the size of a large living room. With astonishment I took in a vast accumulation of stores and equipment, stacked on natural shelves and ledges of rock, or simply on the ground. There were air beds and blankets; huge mounds of tinned food and dry goods; cooking utensils; rows of gas cylinders; drums of paraffin; Tilley lamps, torches, and batteries; kit bags; an armory of guns; rope and caving gear; and—significantly—a pile of motorcar number plates. I could see now why they'd needed that wicker basket. A homelier touch was provided by a small mirror attached to a stalactite at eye level. I took a quick glance in it, and was relieved to see that my facial hair was still in good order.

"Well," Jim said, "I guess we're all hungry. What say we grab a bite?"

9

The cave now took on a strangely domestic aspect. While I rested on one of the air beds, at the fringe of the lighted zone, Rex and Jim set about preparing not just a "bite" but a considerable meal. Rex peeled and shredded onions. Jim took a large saucepan to the stream and scooped up water. Then he picked out tins of meat and vegetables from the store and emptied the ingredients into a saucepan and set it on the ring of a bottled-gas stove.

As they busied themselves with their culinary chores, I studied them as closely as the light allowed. Now that they'd discarded their guns, there was nothing special about them to suggest the ruthless killers and torturers that I knew them to be. There were no marks of Cain. Rex was tall, lean, and darkly good-looking in a craggy way, with a high forehead, a nose with a thin bridge, and a long cleft chin. He could have been the scion of some aristocratic family—and for all I knew, he was. He was more than ever the unmistakable leader in the setup so far—an ironic commentary, I thought, on the total rejection by anarchists of all authority. If they couldn't do without it in a gang of three or four, what was supposed to

136

happen after they'd overthrown society?

Jim had bulk and muscle, with the hunched oxlike shoulders of a campus footballer, and a short, powerful neck. He was physically formidable, but he looked amiable— at least at the moment.

Both men, I guessed, were in their middle or late twenties. Both were dressed, as I was, in casual nondescript jackets and patched, frayed jeans.

While they occupied themselves, I reflected briefly on my own situation—on the unplanned turn of events, and the perils that lay ahead. As far as my appearance was concerned, I had no immediate anxiety. The gang had accepted me as Lacey, they were getting steadily more used to me as Lacey, and they were unlikely now to subject me to any rigorous inspection. The poor light in the cavern was an unexpected stroke of luck, and since they needed to economize on fuel, that luck would probably continue. If I kept away from the immediate vicinity of the Tilley lamp, I should be in no danger visually. Not, at least, unless something happened to arouse their suspicion. . . .

Two things could do that. Behavior, for one—as I'd long realized. I knew virtually nothing about Lacey's relationship with the gang, nothing about his role, little about his attitudes. I might well do or say something that would appear quite out of character for the man they knew. It was a hazard I had to accept, though I could lessen it by being cautious, alert for cues, and sensitive to the tone of the company.

The second danger was much greater. Once we got down to serious talking, as we were bound to do, I'd be on a tightrope with an abyss on either side. To know too little would be as fatal as to know too much. My best hope was that *they* would do most of the talking and telling, which was reasonable enough, since I had supposedly spent the past twelve months shut up in jail, and they had been free and active. But it was going to be a precarious passage. . . .

There was just one item on the other side of the ledger. In the next hour or two, I was bound to learn a great deal about the gang. Enough, perhaps, to insure their ultimate capture—if I ever got away . . .

A savory odor was beginning to rise from the pot. Rex was still peeling onions and throwing them in. Jim was stirring the contents. There were snatches of talk as the preparations went ahead.

Rex said, "Sorry it took us so long to get you out, Chris. There was a lot of planning and organizing to do, and we had to find a safe base to work from. After that, there was all the provisioning. . . . That's why we gave them plenty of time to reply and didn't hurry over the final arrangements—we weren't quite ready."

"I'm not complaining, Rex." I made no comment on the "arrangements." I wasn't supposed to know anything about them, and since I knew everything the subject seemed best left alone. "I don't see how you could have moved any sooner."

Jim said, "Too bad we had to leave you at the factory. I sure felt a heel over that. But I looked back, and there you were on the ground, out cold as far as I could see, and one of the guys was grabbing your gun, and an alarm bell was going off. . . ."

"Don't give it a thought, Jim. You did what was best."

"Well, I guess it wouldn't have helped any if we'd all got clobbered."

"Of course not . . . Did you have any trouble over the getaway?"

"Piece of cake," Rex said. "We switched to the cars we'd left parked, and in minutes we were away in the wide blue yonder."

"With seventy-five grand," Jim said. "Pounds sterling—not bucks. It sure was a good haul."

I nodded. "There was a lot of talk about it in jail. . . . How's the money holding out?"

"Fine. We've topped it up a bit since then. A couple of small jobs. We're credit-worthy."

Rex said, "How's the nosh coming along, Jim?"

Jim peered into the pot. "I'd say it's ready. . . . Come and get it."

He ladled out the stew into enamel dishes, and we sat on our air beds and wolfed it. It was delicious. Afterward we had tinned fruit, processed cheese, and instant coffee. Jim boiled some more water and washed up in a greasy-looking pail, drying the dishes on a graying bit of towel. When he'd finished, he carried the pail across the cavern floor and poured the dirty water into the down-going stream. The used tins were added to an already considerable pile. I wondered if there were any rats in the cave! Rex produced cigarettes—Diplomats, I was glad to see, not pot—and we all lit up. Then we got down to the solid talk that had always been inevitable, the questions and the answers and the reminiscences, and I was out in the minefield.

Rex said, "Where did you pick up the name Tom Lacey, Chris?"

An easy one to start with! If the name had had any associations for the gang, Rex would hardly have asked the question. I said. "It was the first name that came into my head when they asked me. It seemed as good as any other."

He nodded. "How bad was it in jail?"

"Could have been worse, Rex. Not a picnic, though. They're good places to keep out of. . . ." I wondered, belatedly, whether I should have said that. Maybe Rex had some jail experience himself. Maybe Lacey would have known that he had. But it was all right—the comment passed unremarked.

"What was the routine?"

I gave him a rundown of life at Kilhurst, thanking my stars that I'd asked Wallace for a schedule. Filling in with convincing bits of corroborative detail. "I built rocking horses for kids—can you believe that? Did some carving. Played chess with a visiting do-gooder. Read quite a lot—though they were sticky about some of the books I asked for. Usual establishment bastards . . . Boredom was the worst thing. But I knew you'd be working on some plan. That kept me going."

A long speech. Too long for the taciturn Lacey? Apparently not. The two men had been interested, nothing more. No surprised glances. Just a nod of understanding from Rex—and a switch of subject.

"What do you think of our new base, Chris?"

"It's out of this world," I said. "Fantastic! Unbelievable!"

"That's what we think." Rex stroked the back of his head in a complacent gesture. "Of course, we've kept on the old business premises in case we're ever stopped and asked for an address. . . ."

The old business premises? Some cover, obviously. A phony hire-car setup? Window cleaning? Some place with living quarters on the spot? It was maddening not to be able to probe. . . .

"But this place," he went on, "gives us much more than any safe house in a town. No neighbors, no prying eyes—and no need now for sorties. We've laid in enough stores to last for two months, provided we go easy on the fuel and grub. You'll be able to lie low here in absolute safety till the heat's off."

"Fine," I said, though it sounded an appalling prospect. I couldn't imagine that even the real Lacey would have found it at all appealing. Weeks on end of squalid communal life below ground, hemmed in by claustrophobic rock, living and sleeping in the same drab clothes in sleazy conditions, with inadequate light, no fresh food, no fresh air, no exercise, no occupation. Better than jail, perhaps—but only just. "Fear can confine you to a space so small," someone had said, "that you might just as well be in the grave."

"How did you come across this place?" I asked.

"We didn't come across it," Rex said, "We searched for it. It was Eddie who had the idea of a pothole in the first place. He'd read something in the papers about some crazy chap who'd lived in one on his own for a hundred and twenty days. Got on well, apparently—quite enjoyed it. So we snooped around and found a book—Yorkshire Caves and Potholes. The book mentioned the Cauldron, and this cave. It said the system had been explored once, a long time ago, but the present owner of the land had put a ban on public visits. That sounded fairly promising, so we came up here and did our own recce. And we decided the place was just right for us. So bit by bit we brought in our stores and equipment—always at night, of course—and took over."

I said, "What if the owner turned up with a party of potholing friends?"

"They'd be unlucky, wouldn't they! Probably all finish

up in the Cauldron. But it's not very likely. . . . We did have a grouse-shooting party one weekend—Eddie spotted them in the distance when he happened to stick his nose out—but they were no worry to us. As you said, we're out of the world down here."

I gazed around the rock-bound cave. "Couldn't it be a bit of a trap, though, Rex? I mean, if the police ever got wind of strange comings and goings, and checked on the hole. A surprise raid at night when everyone was asleep . . . Do you mount a guard?"

Rex shook his head. "There's no chance of surprise, Chris. The last man in always lowers the top ladder. And at night we lift the big ladder off its hook and keep it down here. That closes the front entrance."

"Is there a back entrance?"

"Well, kind of—though *we* look on it more as an emergency exit, don't we, Jim? We've all explored it. It's a tunnel that starts over there. . . ." Rex pointed vaguely into darkness. "It drops down pretty steeply for about a quarter of a mile and then climbs for another quarter of a mile and comes up in a hollow like the one above us. It's a tight squeeze for about a hundred yards in the middle—not more than two feet by two feet—and there's a tricky place where it branches into three separate tunnels. A bit of a labyrinth, and we got lost there—panic stations for a while! But it's quite manageable when you know it—as long as you're wearing the right gear. Helmets, protective suits, and so on. We could all be out that way in half an hour. If we ever got into real trouble here, it would be a safe escape hatch. I'll show you sometime."

"I'd like to see it," I said. "By the way, where exactly are we? You said Yorkshire. . . ."

"We're on the edge, actually. About four miles northeast

of a small town called Long Kirkdale and the same distance north of a village called Ampleton. We're eighteen hundred feet up. . . . It's all limestone country, of course. Rough, wild, and empty."

"Don't the cars leave tracks when you drive up?"

"Not that anyone would think twice about. The odd wheel mark here and there could have been left by a shooting party or any casual trespasser. For the last half-mile, the surface is mostly bare rock—and everywhere the ground's as hard as iron. . . . What did worry us to start with was the thought of leaving cars out on the open moor—drawing attention, if some bailiff or gamekeeper should happen along. But the Cauldron solved that problem. There are eight cars down there now—and plenty of room for more. Easy come, easy go! When we need another, we take a trip somewhere and lift one from a car park. But now that we're stocked up here we shan't need much transport. Every home comfort right to hand."

"What do you use for a bog?"

"No problem at all," Rex said airily. For a moment I was reminded of George. "All mod cons laid on. Jim fixed it up. No flush, but lots of running water. Not as much as when we first took up residence—that's the drought, of course. But plenty . . . Show the gentleman the loo, Jim."

Jim heaved himself up from his air bed. "Grab yourself a torch," he said, indicating a pile. He took one himself and led the way across the cavern floor, directing his light into the Stygian darkness ahead. The beam soon revealed a break in the surface of the wall: the entrance to another passage, wide and high. Ten yards along it, there was a bend, and just beyond the bend a makeshift canvas structure, a sort of privy tent. Inside the tent there was a bottomless bucket with a seat, carefully sited over a descending stream, which I took to be a continuation of the one in the cave. Jim regarded his creation with pride, while I made brief use of it.

"If you keep going from here," he said, pointing beyond the loo, "you come out at the back exit."

I took a few steps farther along the passage, shining my torch ahead. The uneven floor fell away sharply; the roof bristled with spikes of stalactites; the serrated yellow walls looked as menacing as a tiger's teeth.

"Not exactly inviting, is it?"

"You can say that again! It's a hellhole. What you're looking at is the easy part! Still, it's better than having no line of retreat."

I gave an affirmative grunt and limped back with him to the cave. Rex was fiddling with a small radio and an aerial, but apparently getting nothing. The silence of the place was broken only by the incessant splash and murmur of the stream that ran through it. The sibilance brought back a memory. "Was this where you recorded the first cassette?" I asked.

Almost before the words were out of my mouth, I knew I'd blundered. I clutched George's phial—and waited to see if the mine would explode.

Rex looked up at me—not suspiciously, but with surprise. "Who told you about the cassettes, Chris?"

"The guard who brought me to Moffat," I said. "He was on at me all the time. Did I know this, did I know that? Trying to get a line on you. A real pig. He said they'd had two messages on cassettes, and the first one had had a background of running water, and what about it."

"What did you say?"

"I said maybe someone had left a tap running somewhere! I didn't know what he was on about. I said no one had briefed me in jail about any cassettes. I said I knew nothing about anything. In the end, he gave up."

Rex looked relieved. "I did record a cassette here, as a matter of fact. Never gave a thought to the background . . . Oh, well—even Homer nods!"

I took my hand out of my pocket, and blinked sweat out of my eyes. A near miss, that! Hastily, I changed the subject. "Tell me about Sally Morland, Rex. Was this where you held her?"

He shook his head. "It would have been too difficult to get her down here. Anyway, she'd have learned too much—we wanted to keep the place a secret for after the exchange. . . . We had a much better idea, didn't we, Jim?"

"Sure did, Rex."

"I'm all ears," I said. "Well"—I tapped my left ear—"one and a half, say."

No one smiled. Neither of them ever seemed to smile. If this was anarchism, I reflected, it was a pretty joyless affair.

Rex said, "Jim bought a boat—for cash. A big cabin cruiser, forty feet long. He picked it up on a foreshore in Essex. It was so rotten you could almost poke your finger through the hull, and the engine was only good for scrap. But it was just the job for us. We managed to nurse it to a quiet anchorage in the Crouch, and smuggled Sally Morland aboard the night we picked her up. It was dead easy. Gun in her back—dinghy from the sea wall . . . After that we kept her locked in the forecabin."

"Did she give any trouble?"

"She did to start with," Jim said. "And how! She kept

going on about that neighbor we knocked off in the drive. Used some mighty rough language—not at all ladylike. Lot of spirit—Irish spirit, I guess. A real tough baby—wouldn't cooperate over anything. Spoiled and rich, that dame—but gutsy. . . ."

I began to revise my rather jaundiced view of Sally Morland. For the first time, I took some pleasure in the thought that she was free.

Jim went on, "We pretty well tamed her in the end, though. We gave her a rundown on what would happen to her if she let out a peep from the boat—with plenty of detail; it even scared me!—and she kind of lost her voice after that. Sure, we had someone to watch her all the time. If another boat came near, we were specially careful. . . . She's quite a girl, I'll say that. Hell of a good-looker . . ." He regarded me thoughtfully. "Come to think of it, I'd say we got the worst of the exchange!" This time he did manage a faint grin.

I wanted to ask him about the burning and the scream, but I'd learned my lesson. Instead I said, "She'll have told the police about the boat by now. Isn't there a risk there?"

"None at all," Rex said. "We took care of everything. Jim had a mustache and dark glasses when he handed over the cash for the boat. No names given on either side. No documents signed . . . Sally Morland knew she was on a boat, of course, but she had no idea what boat, or where. Mostly she was kept blindfolded—always unless we were masked. . . . Anyway, before we left for the exchange point, which was this morning before first light, we scuttled the boat. It would have sunk without help before long—but we knocked out a plank and it went down like a stone in sixty feet of water. Never to be heard of again! So you can rest easy, Chris."

"You were always a hell of a good organizer," I said.

"Well, the logistics of the operation *were* pretty tough." Rex stroked the back of his head. "Particularly for Eddie. There's no doubt he bore the brunt. His job was to snatch a suitable van yesterday, drive it up here—change the plates, of course—load the clothes and guns into it ready for the Moffat meeting, park it down near the road for the night, walk down to it this morning, and drive off for Moffat. All of which, it seems, he managed without a hitch. Jim and I had the easy job, once we'd sunk the boat and got Sally ashore. Jim liberated a car from the car park at the local yacht club, and we were away before full daylight. We had twelve hours to kill, so we took it slowly to the Lakes and stopped for an hour or two on the way. I must say it all went off very smoothly."

"Well—congratulations, Rex. You did a great job."

"Don't we always, Chris? *You've* had a hand in a few. . . . Talking of jobs, you haven't seen our latest effort. Come over here for a minute. . . ." He led the way to a remote corner of the cave and shone his torch onto a low crystalline ledge. As I gazed down at the object caught in the light, my skin crawled and I wondered what nameless horror he was going to show me.

The object was a small coffin—perhaps three feet long. A child's coffin. It had brass handles, and was solidly constructed of some expensive wood. "Jim made it," Rex said. "A work of loving care." He raised the lid with a conjuror's flourish. "There—what do you think of that?"

I forced myself to look—then looked more closely. The coffin was almost full of yellowish-white sticks, like candles. There were bits of wiring—and, at one end of the coffin, a clock.

"Nearly fifteen pounds of jelly," Rex said. "And a battery-driven clock. When the lid's closed, you can't hear a sound."

I made an effort to speak calmly. "What's the plan, Rex?"

"We thought we'd leave it in some fashionable church, just before the service. Stick it near the altar, with a velvet runner over it and an arum lily on top. Nobody would be likely to move it. . . . It should scatter the congregation far and wide."

"Brilliant," I said. "Whose idea was it?"

"This one was Irma's."

It was on the tip of my tongue to say "Irma?"—but I checked just in time. . . . So there was a woman member of the gang! And, from Rex's matter-of-fact tone, someone I could be expected to know about.

I said, "How is Irma?"

"She's fine. . . . Eddie and Jim made the bomb, of course. It's our biggest yet. Nearly twice the size of the Blackpool one . . . But perhaps you didn't hear about that?"

Had I heard about it? I couldn't remember. There'd been so many bombs going off in the past few months . . . "No," I said, playing for safety. "We only got some of the news in jail."

"It was a beauty. Not much carnage but a lot of damage."

"You've certainly been busy. . . . Where is Eddie, by the way?"

"He's picking up Irma. We didn't need her for the final jobs, so she went off to Kendal yesterday for a hairdo and a hot bath. She spent the night there." Rex shone his torch on his watch, and frowned. "I can't think what's happened to them—they should have been here long ago. . . ."

He set off back over the crackling floor and I limped along beside him. I felt sick to my stomach at what I'd seen and heard. I didn't think I could take any more. When we reached the lighted area, I said, "What about me having a bit of a kip, Rex? It's been a long day. I'm pretty well all in."

"Why not?" he said. "You've earned it. Make yourself at home."

"Thanks." I drew my air bed a little farther into the shadows, eased Lacey's shoes off my feet, and stretched out.

10

I was tired all right. I wasn't kidding about that. A bad night, an early start, a long drive, a tense encounter, a strenuous climb, and—to cap it all—an hour of sustained impersonation and the shock of the bomb—had left me drained. Sleep, though, was the very last thing I had in mind. What I needed, and what I had gained, was a period of quiet, a chance to consider without interruption how I could escape from this scabrous gang with my life—and with all the vital knowledge of them that I now possessed.

One thing was absolutely clear to me. The escape, if there was to be one, would have to be soon. Already the hair attached to my head and face was troubling me. My own beard was sprouting under the false one. By morning I'd be in acute discomfort—and the gummed-on hair would be getting dangerously tatty. No doubt the gang would expect me to shave it off—the obvious step for a man in hiding whose description would have been circulated nationwide—but that would leave me worse off than ever.

Without my concealing full set, the contours of my face and chin would never pass for Lacey's, even in the half-light of the cave. In short, the impersonation could not be sustained. My survival depended on quick action. Action this night . . . But what action?

For James Bond, the solution of the problem would have presented no difficulties. Rex and Jim had settled down to a game of cards in the circle of light. Their guns were on a ledge beside them. Easy, in theory, to join them after an interval, make some comment on the game, seize one of the guns, and spray them with bullets. Easy for Bond. But I knew nothing about guns, nothing about magazines or safety catches. Those lads would probably get me before I could even find the trigger. It just wasn't my scene. To have any hope of getting out of this mess, I'd got to rely on craft and cunning, not violence.

Could I, I wondered, think up some plausible excuse for temporarily leaving the cave? Something that ruled out any risk of my being quickly pursued? That was vital. My battered feet wouldn't stand a race or a chase. In any break for freedom, I had to be sure of a long start.

I considered various excuses. I could say I was going up for a breath of fresh air. But since, inside the cave, the air was dry and cool, and outside it was hot and stifling, that would cause surprise. I could say I wanted to stretch my legs. But since it was apparent that I could only just manage to hobble across the cavern floor, that also would seem strange. And the last thing I wanted to do was to start a train of suspicion by an obviously phony excuse. I could say I felt claustrophobic in the cave—shut in by rock—worse than prison. Got to get used to it slowly. That might sound more reasonable. Even so, Rex or Jim or both would probably insist on coming with me—if only for my own safety. They wouldn't like the idea of me wandering around in the dark on my own, over unfamiliar ground studded with holes. I could try it—but I doubted if I'd get away with it. . . .

How about stealing up and out during the night, when they were all asleep and dead to the world? That might be possible, if I could avoid those snapping bits of stalagmite on the floor. . . . Then I remembered. Rex had said they took the big ladder down at night. And the clatter of setting it up again—even if I could manage it by torchlight—would be certain to rouse them. . . .

I switched my thoughts to the back exit. The emergency exit. Wasn't that the obvious answer? I'd been shown where the passage started. If the gangsters were asleep, my departure from the cave probably wouldn't be noticed. If by any chance it was noticed, I could say I was going to the loo—naturally, with a torch—and no one would bother. . . . and I could keep going. Down the long tunnel that Rex had described. With luck, even at a limping pace, I could be up on the surface and out of reach before anyone realized that I'd gone.

With luck. But could I count on luck? I'd no experience of potholing, no expertise. I'd have no helmet or protective clothing against the tearing limestone. There might be drops to negotiate—and I'd have no equipment. . . . Even the entrance had looked hideously uninviting. And there was the hundred yards of narrow pipe that Rex had mentioned. Two feet by two feet, he'd said. Not even crawling room—it would be belly stuff. Suppose I got caught up on something? Suppose I got stuck? And then there were those other tunnels that branched off and led nowhere. It would be a tossup whether I took the right one. I could easily lose myself in the hellhole. The torch would fail,

151

and I'd be helpless. Had I the nerve to attempt it? I doubted it. Mentally and physically I shrank from the prospect. . . . But had I any choice? Wasn't it the best bet? Perhaps the only bet . . . And if the worst came to the worst, there was always George's phial.

I was still, in imagination, making the horrific passage down the tunnel when a loud reverberation through the cave brought me bolt upright on the air bed. Rex looked up, unperturbed, from his cards. "It's Eddie and Irma," he said. "That was their van going down the Cauldron—it always makes a din in here. . . . Had a good kip?"

"Too short," I said, "but better than nothing."

In a few moments, footsteps sounded above. Voices became audible. Someone switched on the top platform light. Figures showed above the ladder. A girl looked over the edge of the precipice. She had long blond hair, and was holding an overnight bag. *"Chris!"* she cried excitedly.

Rex called, "Cool it, Irma. Watch your step!"

She was on the ladder, bag and all, and coming down fast. At the bottom she ran to me. "Chris! Darling Chris! Oh, how wonderful to see you!" She threw her arms round my neck and covered my lips and beard and mustache with passionate kisses—which, confused though I was, it seemed diplomatic to return.

11

Eddie came down more cautiously, the guns he'd taken from George and Shafto slung across his back. He stacked them in the armory and wiped sweat from his forehead with the sleeve of his jacket. "Well, we finally got here!" He sounded pretty exhausted, which in view of the day he'd had, was hardly surprising.

Rex said, "What kept you, Eddie? We expected you hours ago."

"We blew a tire, Rex—just outside Kendal. Had to change the wheel in the dark—and the bloody nuts were tight. We had the hell of a job."

"I was furious," Irma said. "Just when I wished to hurry to meet Chris." She had a slight guttural accent—German, I thought, or Central European—but her voice was low and seductive.

"Ah, well," Rex said, "we're all here now, safe and sound. We've got Chris back, and our problems are over. I'd say this calls for a celebration. How about it, Jim?"

"Sure . . ." Jim went to a stores shelf behind the panto-mime scenery and presently emerged with a trayload of bottles and tumblers, which he set down on the floor. "Now—what's yours, Chris? The usual?"

I said, "That sounds odd, Jim, after a year. My 'usual' would be a mug of cocoa, if I was lucky. . . . But, yes, thanks."

Jim started to pour the drinks. Eddie foraged for food, and came up with biscuits and cheese. Irma, when momentarily she had stopped hugging and kissing me, clasped one of my hands and gently stroked the palm with her fingertips. Despite the uncertain light, I could see that she was very well shaped and—apart from a small tight mouth—good-looking. She couldn't have been much more than twenty.

We took our drinks. Mine turned out to be a very small rum-and-water—and I wished it was larger. Jim's seemed to be gin-and-tonic. Eddie and Rex had beer, and Irma a

Coke. Whatever else they were, they didn't appear to be heavy drinkers. No vices, really—apart from an addiction to murder.

Rex raised his glass. "Well, here's to the underground movement!"—and we all drank. Irma was still clinging to me with her free hand as though she'd never let me go.

Eddie drained his beer in a single long draught. "That's better," he said. "God, it's hot up top." He was standing in the circle of light, and I saw now that he had a squint. He'd looked better in sunglasses. "Nearly eleven o'clock," he said, glancing at his watch, "and it's still like a sauna out there." He rummaged for a towel and soap and went off with a torch toward the loo.

Irma nuzzled my chest, cuddled me, pressed her breasts against me. "Darling!" She stood on tiptoe and whispered in my ear. "Let us go to bed. Now! I cannot wait." It was a pretty loud whisper, audible to one and all.

No one smiled. No one seemed surprised. Rex said, "Go on, Chris—take her off and give her the works."

I fought down something very close to panic. I'd as soon have made love to a cobra—but that wasn't the problem. There are things no man can safely impersonate, and one of them is another man in bed. Like fingerprints, no two are the same. An intimate session with Lacey's German girl friend would start and end with exposure.

I said, "Let's leave it till tomorrow, Irma. I've had a tough day and I'm pretty tired."

"Tonight, Chris! Now! I will make you less tired. At first! Afterwards, more tired. Then you can sleep." She gave a throaty laugh, and ran a hand down me from shoulder to crotch. "Come!"

I looked around, trying to stall. "It's sort of public here, darling."

"The bedroom is on the first floor," Irma said. "We have nice sand, an air bed, a light—and me. What more can you ask?"

"I really am too tired. . . ."

Rex said, "Oh, come on, Chris, make an effort. You've had a kip—and she's been waiting for you for a year."

Somehow I doubted that. A year, in this communal atmosphere, with three vigorous young men around? I might be first among equals, perhaps—no more. . . . But that wasn't the point. I looked up in desperation at the "bedroom," the place where my fate would be sealed. And suddenly, belatedly, I saw it as a way to salvation. A horrible, brutal way—but did I now have any alternative?

I gave in with a sigh. "Okay, darling," I said. "You've talked me into it. Lead me to the boudoir."

12

She slipped away briefly into the darkness and emerged moments later in some kimono-like garment that stopped well short of her ankles. The men were no longer paying any attention to us. Eddie, back from his ablutions, had got himself another beer and was watching Rex and Jim at their resumed card game. I followed Irma up the ladder to the sandy alcove.

She switched on the electric lamp. It looked a powerful

lamp, but the light that came from it was far from brilliant.
"I think it needs a new battery, Chris."

I said, "So do I."

She laughed.

I took off my jacket, for greater freedom. She seized
my hands, and ran caressing fingers up my arms to the
sleeves of the T-shirt, and down again. Suddenly she
paused. "Chris, what has happened to your mole?"

"It began to itch," I told her. "Kept me awake at night.
So I got the prison doctor to take it off."

I spoke casually, but with an inward *frisson*, as she explored the tiny scar. Was it exactly in the right place?
Would she remember?

"I am sorry," she said. "I was accustomed to your mole.
Still, it was not the most important part of you!"

She lay down on the air bed, letting the kimono fall
away. She was naked, and quite shameless. Her breasts
were lovely. Her shapely thighs were invitingly apart. Her
blond hair, faintly scented, framed her face. In the language of the day, she was a dish. By Lacey, to be partaken
of . . .

I knelt beside her, as amorous as a polar icecap. I knew
exactly what I had to do. Her neck was slim, my hands
were strong. I didn't have to kill her, not if I could help
it—even though, for that bomb alone, she deserved it. All
I had to do was squeeze her throat till she was senseless.
If she made any sound, her friends would put it down
to the ecstasies of love. Followed by the silence of satiated
sleep . . . After that, I could be out of the cave in minutes,
with a long start.

There was only one trouble. *I couldn't do it.* I knew that
my life depended on it. I knew that I was being irrationally
soft. But now that the moment had come, I just could

not dig my thumbs into her throat and throttle her to unconsciousness and perhaps to death.

She gave an impatient cry as I stared down at her. "Chris, be quick! Take off your clothes. . . . Hurry!"

I seemed to have no choice. I stripped off, slowly, to my underpants. I began to shiver. It wasn't the cold of the cave that had set my teeth chattering—it was the touch of icy fear, the sense that the charade was almost over. . . . But it was the cold that suddenly gave me a second glimpse of salvation.

"It's no good," I said. "You look wonderful—but I can't make love when I'm frozen. Isn't there a blanket anywhere?"

"We do not need a blanket. I will warm you." She reached for me, and I drew back. She pulled the kimono around her in a petulant gesture. "Very well—go and get a blanket. There are plenty in the cave. Rex will show you."

I bent and kissed her—a lover's kiss, with an actor's passion. And coaxed her, "Be an angel, darling, and get it for me. That ladder is difficult for me."

"Why?"

"I hurt my foot in prison. My ankle. Every time I get on the ladder, I'm afraid I shall fall."

She pouted. "I think you are not the man you were."

How right she was!

I kissed her again. "Fetch the blanket, and I will show you that I am. It will be like old times."

She looked at me uncertainly. She was uneasy and I knew why. I was being out of character for the Lacey she remembered. The knife edge, now . . . Then she said, "All right, I will get your silly blanket." She drew the kimono around her, tying the cord, and went quickly to the ladder and down to the cave. I heard her say to the cardplayers, "He is cold!" No one laughed.

I moved to the precipice edge, my heart pounding. If I failed now, there'd be nothing left but the cyanide. I gripped the top of the ladder, heaved it off the piton, and pulled upward and backward with all my strength. For a moment it held. Then I felt something give way at the bottom, there was a jangle of metal—and the ladder was up in the air, at right angles. I hauled it in and stepped back out of sight as Rex suddenly shouted, "Hi, what the hell's going on?"

I got back into my clothes, ignoring the confused and mounting din below, and groped my way along the pitch-dark passage to the entrance hole. I found the short ladder by stumbling over it. Eddie had pulled it down behind him. I set it up against the limestone wall and climbed out onto the moor.

13

The first thing I did was to shed Lacey's shoes. I was surprised that I still had them on. I must have had them on when I was kneeling beside Irma's naked body in my underpants. Ludicrous! I began to laugh. A fragment of Churchill's *Marlborough* shot into my mind. "My lord, home from the wars, pleasured me in his boots three times before breakfast." I laughed louder and louder. I knew it was hysteria. The danger was past, but nothing was funny. Still, I had to laugh. When you expect to die, and somehow live, it's hilarious.

After the paroxysm was over, I tried to consider the new situation calmly.

By now, the gang would know that they had been deceived, penetrated, and uncovered. They would know their peril. They would be in a desperate hurry to leave the cave. They would know there was no way they could climb that forty-foot overhang without a ladder. Probably they were already making for the back exit. They'd done it once, they could do it again. A half-hour trip to the surface, Rex had said. . . .

What I had to do was get in touch with George. Tell him everything I could about them. They'd be out of the cave long before the police could reach the moor—but now, with the detailed information I could give, their ultimate capture was a near certainty. . . . I needed civilization, a telephone. Urgently. But where to find it, on this black night in the hills?

The moon had disappeared. There was a menacing bank of cloud, such as I hadn't seen in months, slowly obliterating the stars. The night was hot, and still, and growing darker every minute, and I had no idea which way to go. No sense of direction at all.

I could think of only one thing. Go downhill. If it's civilization you're after, go downhill.

I stepped out gingerly in my socks. Walking was painful, but it was a lot better without Lacey's shoes. There were sharp stones underfoot, but the pressure was off. I moved forward with caution, mindful of the invisible Cauldron, testing every step. This moor could be as full of holes as a Gruyère cheese.

Presently I came to a dip, a gulley. Now which way, if any, was down? In the blackness, it was impossible to tell. Or was it? I was suddenly aware that my socks were wet. I fumbled at the rough ground. There was a trickle of water in the bottom of the gulley—a moving dampness, perhaps from a spring. That was what I needed—running water to guide me. "Even the weariest river winds somewhere safe to sea." I kept going, downhill. It was a tough passage in the total darkness. An inch-by-inch affair, with every step a hazard. Sometimes the bed of the gulley fell sharply away in front of me, and I had to negotiate a rocky, precipitous drop by feel, blind. It was risky, but not scary. This was a natural challenge that I knew I could meet. From the creatures behind me, and all their deviltry, I was unbelievably, sublimely, safe and free. . . .

A sudden crash of thunder startled me. There was a stab of forked lightning that seemed to pierce the ground almost at my feet. The long-awaited storm. The three months awaited storm . . . A freak wind roared past me, carrying bits of flying vegetation with it—and as quickly died. There was another peal of thunder. Then the rain started.

I had never known such rain. It wasn't the ordinary hard pencils of water. It was slabs of water. A deluge of water. The black sky tipping up and emptying out.

In a matter of minutes, my gulley was a rushing stream. This must be what they called a flash flood. The ground everywhere was so hard that nothing could soak in. The water was running off it as though from a sheet of metal.

The thunder cracked louder and nearer; the flashes of lightning were almost continuous. I welcomed them, for they showed me in vivid brilliance all the hazards on my way. Soaked beyond troubling, I plunged and staggered down. Down, down, and down—downhill all the way. At one brief moment, through the curtain of rain and between flashes, I thought I saw a light below me, man-made, not Nature's. It gave me hope. It could be a car on a road, or a house. . . .

Incredibly, the rain grew heavier. Water was pouring down the slopes of the moor as over a great weir. At times I felt near to drowning as waves of rain washed over my face. The din was deafening. The stabbing forks of lightning seemed to be aimed at me personally. There was a mounting roar of water all around me. I had no choice but to go along with it—and soon the weight of it carried me off my feet. I was flung violently against something solid—the root of a tree?—and I grabbed it. It gave way, and I felt myself being swept down, down, by an irresistible force. I was in the gulley again, but now it was brimming, a raging torrent. I stopped struggling and let myself go. I was on a Cresta Run of water. I had the sensation of enormous speed, of being lifted and carried. It was almost pleasurable. . . . Then I blacked out.

14

I surfaced reluctantly from the drowsy comfort of semi-consciousness. I was in bed. I was in bed in a small room. I turned my head toward a subdued light. Daylight through curtained windows . . . I turned away. I was aware of pain. Pain around my mouth. Pain in the head. Pain in an arm. Pain in my feet.

Someone was moving quietly. Someone in white and blue. I focused on the moving figure. A nurse, surely . . .

She came to the bedside, fingered my wrist. "How do you feel?"

"Fine," I said—an all-time lie. But at least I was beginning to remember, in a hazy kind of way.

"I'll get Sister," she said.

Gingerly, I explored myself. My left hand and forearm were in plaster. My right foot seemed to be bandaged. I had some sort of bandage round my chin. My beard and mustache had gone. So had my wig. The pain wasn't too bad. They must have doped me. . . .

Now there was someone else by the bed. Sister? Tall, thin, severe . . .

I said, "What happened? How did I get here?"

"You were found at the bottom of Clear Ghyll when the storm died down. Close to the edge of the road. A motorist happened to spot you. . . . You're very lucky to be alive."

"Yes," I said, "I am!"

"Where had you been? What were you doing?" She didn't sound at all like a ministering angel.

"I was up on the moors. I was washed down in the storm. . . . How much am I damaged?"

"A fractured wrist, badly lacerated feet, a gash on your chin, and slight concussion . . . Do you remember your name? We don't know who you are." She looked at me with hard suspicion.

"Where am I?"

"The cottage hospital, Long Kirkdale . . . What is your name?" Her tone had sharpened.

All that false hair, of course! And probably they'd found George's phial in the pocket of my jacket. Not exactly a routine patient.

"Farran," I said. "Robert Farran . . . . What day is it?"

"Sunday."

162

"Sunday!" Somehow I struggled into a sitting position. When I'd escaped from the cave, it had been Friday. "I must speak on the telephone."

"Later, Mr. Farran. You still need rest."

"Now . . . I'm in Government service. It's a matter of life and death. For God's sake, take me to a telephone."

Her fingers strayed to my pulse. I saw her nod to the nurse. The nurse went out. She was back in a few minutes, with a telephone on a long lead. I grabbed it.

What the hell was the number? That vital number. I struggled to concentrate. Ah, yes . . . I got the operator—and in the end I got the number.

A woman answered. "Yes? Who is it?" A businesslike voice, giving nothing away.

"This is Bob Farran. I want George."

"Mr. Farran! Well, heaven be praised. Hold on—he's right here."

George came on the line. "Dear boy!" he said.

"Listen, George . . ." I told him, in the fewest possible words, all he needed to know. I was still a bit muzzy, so it wasn't the most coherent report in the world, but his encouraging grunts showed that he was broadly getting the message. I told him where I was. I outlined what had happened to me. I told him the approximate whereabouts of the pothole. Near the Devil's Cauldron—marked on the map. I told him about the gang of four. The bomb. The back exit. "They'll have left long ago," I said, "but you might still catch up with them." I gave him short descriptions of Rex and Jim, Eddie and Irma. I assured him there wasn't much wrong with me. "That's all, George. See you. Good hunting!"

I hung up, and sank back on the bed, completely spent

by the effort. The last thing I saw before I closed my eyes was the nurse's face. She was pretty, like Irma—but she had a generous mouth, and she was kind. "It's lovely here," I said, and went to sleep.

15

By next morning, apart from the nuisance of the bandages, I was feeling comparatively normal. I ate a hearty one-handed breakfast, and glanced through a newspaper. A friendly doctor, accompanied by the Matron, paid me a brief visit and said I would live. Sister looked in once or twice during the morning. She had noticeably thawed toward me—indeed, she was quite motherly—and she asked no more questions. Someone, evidently, had convinced her that my disguise had had no criminal significance and that Robert Farran, despite appearances to the contrary, was a respectable citizen. I guessed that Mr. Fixit had been discreetly at work, but I didn't probe.

Around midday, George showed up in person, which didn't entirely surprise me. He said all the appropriate things—like "Thank God you're alive, dear boy," and "We'd almost given up hope," and "How are you feeling now?"—gripping my undamaged hand. He was in a great hurry to get back on the job, so we didn't talk for long, but he asked a few pertinent questions and I filled him in on some details of my time in the cave that I thought might be useful to him in tracing the gang. He told me that the pothole had been located, and would be thoroughly searched for clues, and that all the resources of the police were being deployed in the hunt for the terrorists. He'd be in touch again, he said, as soon as he had any news.

My thoughts ranged widely during that day of comparative peace and leisure. I looked back with some astonishment at the dramatic events since Moffat. I recalled with photographic clarity the tense moments of the exchange on the col, the furious drive to the pothole, the car going over into the Cauldron, the cave itself, and the difficult scene with Irma when all was in the balance. I wondered, a little wryly, if maybe I'd get a postcard of thanks from Frank Morland in lieu of the quarter of a million pounds he owed me. I wondered how Sally Morland was making out after her ordeal. But most of all I thought about the gang, and what an extraordinary phenomenon of the age they were.

What struck me most forcibly about them, looking back, was their total lack of overt passion. They reminded me of John Wyndham's Midwich Cuckoos: they looked human, but they seemed to have no ordinary human emotions—not even hatred. As bloody-minded conspirators, they were at the top of the league; as ideologues, they were way down. I had heard, during my time with them, no philosophical word, no hint of revolutionary idealism, no enthusiasm for their cause. They had seemed entirely uninterested in the new heaven that was presumably the goal of their destructive acts. They had given no hint of a world of the mind. Their outward interest had been solely in the mechanics of their operations, the competence of their planning. It was as though, having once decided on their course, they had never again given its purpose a single thought. I saw them, in retrospect, as sick delinquents, conscienceless misfits enjoying the exercise of a godlike power. If there was anything weightier behind their violence, perhaps it would emerge when they were caught.

If they were caught . . . Because of the accident of the storm, and my whole lost day and a half, they'd had a far longer start than they should have had. Of course, they could have had their own difficulties on the rain-swept moor. After that, they'd have had to find transport. They'd have had to improvise some plan. . . . Had they, I wondered, made for those former premises that Rex had spoken of without indicating where they were? Or would they have dispersed? That seemed more likely. As a group, they'd be much more easily identifiable from my descriptions than they would as individuals. Perhaps by now they were all out of the country. A gang like that would be sure to have false passports hidden away somewhere. . . .

Their capture, I belatedly realized, was far from being just the hope of a law-abiding citizen. It was now of vital personal concern to me. I had made a stupid mistake in giving my real name at the hospital, and if I hadn't been half doped I'd never have done it. The plan had always been to keep my identity a secret. The news was bound to get out, sooner or later, that a man with a lot of false red hair had been washed down from the moor on the night of the storm, and I couldn't imagine Rex failing to put two and two together if the information ever reached him. From that point, if he was at liberty, it would be only a step to getting the name Robert Farran. And only one more step to getting Robert Farran himself! So I wasn't out of the wood yet. . . .

However, in the late afternoon that faintly nagging anxiety was dramatically set at rest. A message arrived from George, hastily scribbled on the back of an envelope and delivered at the hospital by a man on a motorcycle. It said: "The wicked have ceased from troubling. We have them all! I'm on my way to you. G."

16

He turned up just as dusk was falling that evening. He was wearing Wellingtons and some old slacks, thickly coated with mud, and I could tell by his gray face and the way he slumped onto the chair by the bed that he'd had a grueling day.

"You got my note?" he asked.

"I did, indeed. And a tremendous relief it was!"

He nodded.

"A big surprise, too. I didn't for a moment expect such quick results. What happened? Where did you pick them up?"

"In the cave, dear boy."

I stared at him in astonishment. "You mean they'd *stayed* there!"

"They had no choice," George said. "They were dead."

"*Dead!*"

"All four of them. We found their bodies jammed in the first few yards of the exit tunnel. They'd been drowned. The whole place must have filled up like a bath when the storm broke. They hadn't a hope."

I said "Oh," and was silent for a while. It wasn't that I had any sentimental feelings about their fate—far from it. But it *was* my hand that had pulled up the ladder, and

I couldn't imagine I would ever get any joy from the recollection. . . .

"Have you recovered the bodies?" I asked.

"Yes . . . Is it all right to smoke here?"

"Go ahead. I haven't felt like it myself, but it's allowed. There's an ashtray beside you."

He lit up. "We had quite a job—there was still some water about. We got the last one up this evening."

"So now you'll be able to discover who they were."

"I'm afraid not," George said. He drew hard on his cigarette. "Ever heard of keelhauling? A barbarous maritime practice in the bad old days. Hauling a malefactor along the bottom of a ship. Scraping him against the barnacles. If he emerged alive, he was in ribbons. . . . These four are in ribbons."

I looked at him in horror. "How? Why?"

"The rush of water into the cave and the tunnel. The sharp knife edges of the rock. To and fro . . . Of course, we've got their belongings. Stores, guns, coffin, gelignite, personal effects—such as they were. Everything will be looked into. But those four will certainly never be identified by their physical remains—and my guess is we shall never know who they were."

I was silent again—recoiling at second hand from what George had seen at first hand. Finally I said, "Or what made them do it."

George gave a twisted smile. "Happily, no! By the mercy of Providence, we shall be spared histories of youthful deprivation and the theories of psychologists. . . . Now I must go—I'm commanded to be in London tonight. But I shall probably see you again tomorrow. Sleep in peace, dear boy."

17

When he returned on the following morning, he looked a different man. The cloak-and-dagger operative had changed into the top civil servant. He was very spruce again, very well tailored, in black jacket and striped trousers. He had the appearance and bearing of an important emissary, which, indeed, he proved to be.

He came briskly to the point. "The Top Man is going to make a statement in the House tomorrow," he said. "A statement that I'm sure he's looking forward to, since for once there'll be no criticism, only plaudits. Mrs. Morland safe and free. No exchange of Lacey. A ruthless gang destroyed. Firm action vindicated. The nation's debt to a courageous young actor. Cheers from all sides of the House. Order papers waved. You can fill in the gaps. . . . The thing is—since, by a timely act of God, all danger for you has passed—the P.M. would like to identify you. What do you say?"

I thought about it—briefly. There were pros and cons—but who at such a moment would be deterred by the cons? "I've no objection," I said. "Very decent of him."

"It will mean tremendous publicity." George's tone was cautionary.

"Good," I said. "I'll enjoy a little top billing for a change."

"A press conference, to start with. Do you feel up to it?"

"I think so. I'm told I don't rate a bed here any more. . . . Shall I have your support at the conference?"

"Of course, dear boy—at a discreet distance. I'm still attached to you." He smiled. "In a professional way . . . On that basis, may I give you a little advice?"

"Didn't you always?"

"Apart from your appearance at the press conference, I think you'd be wise to go into retreat for a day or two. If you don't, you'll have no peace—the reporters will follow you like a cloud of hornets."

I saw his point. "What do you suggest?"

"A good hotel and a temporary pseudonym."

"Who'll pay?"

"The taxpayer."

"Then I accept with pleasure."

"Good . . . Of course, there'll be people you'll *want* to hear from. We could put someone in your flat to monitor your phone calls and take messages. Then pass the word on to you. How does that appeal?"

"You think of everything, George. . . . The caretaker has a key."

He patted my plastered wrist. "There'll be a car here for you at eleven tomorrow morning," he said.

18

The hotel proved to be one of London's finest. George was waiting for me in the foyer, ready to assist me to the lift after I'd checked in as "John Elliott." I felt like an out-of-season skiing casualty, but at least my various bandages made it certain that no one would recognize me as Robert Farran.

I was given a magnificent penthouse suite overlooking the Park—the sort of place that only a sheik or the taxpayer could afford. There were masses of flowers in the sitting room, and a cabinet full of drinks, and TV and hi-fi, and two brand-new suitcases with the initials "J. E." containing a variety of clothes and personal belongings that had been collected from my flat.

I listened to a résumé of the Prime Minister's statement and panegyric on the six-o'clock news. Modesty forbids me to record a word of it. Most of the extended news bulletin dealt with various aspects of the story, and all of it was flattering. I felt thankful that I had followed George's advice and gone temporarily into hiding. Reaction was setting in after all the excitement, and I didn't feel like talking to anyone. I had a couple of drinks and a gourmet dinner served in my room, and went to bed early.

Like Byron after *Childe Harold*, I woke next morning to find myself famous.

The first message that reached me through George's sieve came around ten o'clock. Would I care to ring John Borley, my agent?

I rang him. He was almost incoherent with excitement.

"Bob, it's fantastic. You can't imagine. How are you? You must have had a hell of a time. I do congratulate you. It's all quite incredible. To think I fell for that lumbago stuff! Bob, they're beating a path to my door. Offers of every kind—I'm snowed under. World Syndicate want to pay you a hundred thousand dollars for your exclusive story. They're waving a check at me right now—ten thousand dollars on account. Shall I take it?"

"Take it," I said. "I can use it."

"When can you sign?"

"Oh—tomorrow or the next day. And we'll talk about any other offers when we meet. I'll ring you. I'm in a bit of a tizzy at the moment."

"I can imagine. . . . There's just one thing, Bob. I hear there's to be a press conference. Don't say too much. Keep it short. An exclusive is an exclusive."

"Understood," I said. "I'm not in a very chatty mood, anyway."

All the same, I felt pretty cheerful as I hung up. It looked now as though I wouldn't even miss Morland's nonexistent money. I was on my own feet again.

19

Before the press conference, George gave me more advice. Or, to be accurate, my orders . . . There was to be no identification of himself by name or description. He would be referred to only as my "liaison officer." There was to be no identification of Shafto. The guards who had accompanied me to Moffat and the exchange point would be merely "police officers." There was to be no mention of the Magic Eye in the prison cell, or of the prison visitor Grenfell, or of my "trial run." No mention of the Chelsea studio, or the St. John's Wood setup, or the guarded clinic. No mention of the cyanide phial. In fact, there was a long list of taboos. . . . Something more might be allowed, George said, when I came to write my story, though everything would have to be carefully vetted. I didn't jib at the prohibitions, and mentally added a few of my own. There were aspects of the story that I had no desire to dwell on.

The conference took place in some country house near London. I was whisked down there, and whisked back, and I never bothered to ask exactly where it was. George had laid it all on, of course, with his customary efficiency, but in the presence of the press he stayed well in the background, just one of several supporting officials. A man from some Ministry, who introduced himself to me as Mr. Dolphin, acted as my chairman.

I enjoyed the conference. Compared with a gang of armed kidnappers, a gang of newsmen and photographers seemed less than formidable. I ducked a few questions "on security grounds," but I gave them enough to satisfy them. I told them about my visit to the Yard. I told them a little about my preparations to pass as Lacey. I told them about Moffat, and the exchange on the col. I told them how Lacey's shoes had upset my escape plans. I told them, at some length, about the different members of the gang, and about my time in the cave, and about the storm on the moor. When they asked me how I'd managed to get away, I said I'd shinned up the ladder when no one was looking. I didn't mention the Irma episode. Somehow I didn't want to talk about her. And I didn't mention Morland. They asked me why I had done it. I said the adventure had appealed to me. . . .

The chairman closed the proceedings after fifty minutes, and the newsmen faded away, their notebooks adequately filled and their cameras stuffed with pictures of the bandaged hero. And George drove me back to the hotel.

20

That evening, Sally Morland came to see me.

She had telephoned my flat, and George's custodian there had telephoned me, and I'd made an appointment for six o'clock in my hotel suite.

I wasn't entirely sure that I wanted to see her. Considering the way Morland had behaved, I thought it could turn out an embarrassing meeting. But I was curious to hear what she had to say—and anyway, in all the circumstances, I could hardly refuse.

She arrived just after six. We shook hands, and for a moment studied each other—I suppose with equal interest. The newspaper photographs I'd seen had done less than justice to her. She was a tall woman, and very graceful. Her dark hair was rich and abundant, her eyes were a delicate shade of blue, and she had a lovely complexion. I was surprised to see how young she looked. She seemed hardly more than a girl, even if she was twenty-five. Her appearance quite disarmed me.

I said, rather fatuously, "We've already met, of course," recalling our brief encounter on the col. She smiled at that, a dimpled smile that for a moment took all the strain from her face.

I suggested drinks, and she chose sherry. I poured sherry for both of us, and sat down in a chair opposite her. We were neither of us entirely at ease.

"Well," I said, raising my glass, "here's to survivors!"

She nodded gravely, and sipped her sherry. "I hope

you're making a good recovery, Mr. Farran." She eyed my bandages.

"Very good, thank you. I look a mess, I know, but it's all quite superficial. . . . How about you? You've had a pretty traumatic experience."

"Yes, it was horrible—and very frightening. But I'm all right now. A bit shaken, that's all."

"No more than that? I expected to see *you* with a bandage, too."

She shook her head. "I suppose you're thinking of the cassette? But it wasn't I who screamed. I wasn't even there when the tape was made. It must have been Irma, putting on a convincing act."

I'd never thought of that—but of course it made sense. They'd have wanted to keep Sally in good condition for the hike to the col. Burning her could have wrecked their plan. . . .

"Well, it's good news," I said. "That tape was enough to freeze the marrow."

"I know—George played it over to me." She was silent for a moment. "I had to see you, Mr. Farran. To thank you. For all you did for me."

I couldn't, in honesty, let that pass. I said, "It wasn't for you, Mrs. Morland. At first, as you probably know, it was for filthy lucre."

"Which, before you set off, you knew you weren't going to get. . . . George has told me what happened."

"For a veteran operator," I said, "George talks too much."

"Only when he thinks it's necessary . . . He's a very fair man."

I couldn't argue with that.

"Okay," I said, "no money . . . But it was still a self-regarding thing. A matter of personal pride, if you like. A challenge. Something to occupy me. I was in poor shape—and work's a catharsis. *I* don't know—anyway, I did it for myself. . . . But of course that doesn't mean I'm not delighted that you've been safely restored to your husband."

It wasn't a kind thing to say, but Morland's conduct still rankled. And, for all her gratitude and sympathy, I couldn't forget that she was Morland's wife.

She looked directly at me. "Restored, yes—but not to my husband."

"Oh?" The interrogative hung in the air.

"I'm divorcing him," she said. "Not because of the financial mess he's got himself into—though they say there may be criminal charges as well. Not because of the outrageous way he treated you. They're just extras. I made up my mind a year ago. . . ."

I waited. I knew now why she had come. She had come to dissociate herself. And to explain.

She went on, in a matter-of-fact tone, "I thought he was terrific when I married him. And in many ways he was. He seemed to have—oh, so many qualities—force, and courage and self-confidence. And great charm. And of course he had money. I'm afraid I was dazzled by the idea of having limitless money. And not just that . . . It's an overwhelming thing to be courted by a man whose name is known and respected all over the country. And I was very young. I really was swept off my feet. . . . Then, soon after our marriage, I began to discover unsuspected things about him. About his character . . ."

She paused again.

"There was a lack of integrity. Everyone knows about that now. But that wasn't all. He—well, he just liked women. He could never stop flitting from flower to flower. And he seemed to lose interest in me. It was a miserable, humiliating time. In the end, I decided we'd have to break up. I wasn't going to stay tied to a man who felt no ties for me—not even affection. He didn't object, but he asked me to wait until after the next election. His majority is very small, you see. And he's very ambitious. Even in these days, a divorce can mean lost votes. It was stupid of him to behave as he did—public men should never be womanizers. . . . Still, I didn't want to be his executioner. I didn't want to ruin his career. So I said I'd wait, and we separated, and I went to live in the country and kept up appearances. . . . Now he's ruined his career himself—so there's nothing more to wait for. That's all. Forgive me for talking so much about myself, Mr. Farran, but I did want to put the record straight."

"I'm very sorry," I said. And I was. One way and another, she seemed to have had more than her fair share of trouble.

"Oh, well, it's been water under the bridge for a long time now. I just wanted you to know."

I got up, and refilled our sherry glasses. And determinedly changed the subject. "Is George still keeping you under wraps?" I asked.

"Not after today—not now the story's out. I think he's arranging something for the press tomorrow. I can't say I'm looking forward to it, but George says it has to happen, so I might as well get it over."

"He's a wise old bird. And I assure you there's nothing to be scared of. You'll find the newsmen most friendly— and as they tend to fire their questions all at the same time, it's easy to pick the ones you want to answer."

"I'll remember that."

"Perhaps you'd like to rehearse what you're going to tell them? I'd very much like to hear your half of the story—that is, if it won't upset you to talk about it. So far, I've only the sketchiest idea what happened to you."

"I'd like to ask *you* a few questions, too," she said.

Suddenly, we were launched on our recollections—the interlocking memories of two strangers whose lifelines had dramatically crossed. Time passed unnoticed. Unnoticed, that is, until I began to feel hungry. Then I said, "I wonder if you'd care to have dinner with me, Mrs. Morland? They'll bring it up here. It would be a great pleasure for me—and we still have so much to talk about. . . . I'm terribly interested in Turkish chickweed!"

She laughed. "I'd like it very much," she said.

We had a most enjoyable dinner and a most absorbing evening together and . . .

But that's the beginning of another story.

Geoffrey Household

RED ANGER

A young English clerk fakes his own suicide to escape a boring job—then reappears as a Romanian refugee from a Russian trawler fleet. From the moment Adrian Gurney, alias Ionel Petrescu, is "discovered" on the coast, however, he is caught in a sinister and unexpected intrigue: He is recruited to hunt down Alwyn Rory, fugitive and reputed traitor. Gurney manages to locate Rory's hiding place, and the two soon find themselves on the run together, as the C.I.A., the K.G.B., and M.I.5 close in.

ROGUE MALE

His mission was revenge, and revenge means assassination. In return he'll be cruelly tortured, tracked by secret agents, followed by the police, relentlessly pursued by a ruthless killer. They'll hunt him like a wild beast, and to survive he'll have to think and live like a rogue male. "A tale of adventure, suspense, even mystery, for whose sheer thrilling quality one may seek long to find a parallel . . . and in its sparse, tense, desperately alive narrative it will keep, long after the last page is finished, its hold from the first page on the reader's mind"—*The New York Times Book Review*.

WATCHER IN THE SHADOWS

Watcher in the Shadows is the story of a manhunt, of a protracted duel fought out in London and the English countryside by two of the most accomplished and deadly intelligence officers to have survived World War II. One of them is a Viennese who served in the British Intelligence; the other is a dangerous fanatic who has already murdered three men. "A thriller of the highest quality"—Anthony Boucher, *The New York Times Book Review*.

Also:
DANCE OF THE DWARFS
HOSTAGE: LONDON

Michael Innes

AN AWKWARD LIE

Bobby, son of that great master of detection Sir John Appleby, finds a body on a golf course. As he wonders what to do, a very attractive girl arrives. When Bobby returns after calling the police, however, the girl has gone . . . and so has the corpse!

CANDLESHOE

What mysterious treasure lies hidden in the dark heart of Candleshoe Manor? And what breath-catching adventures will unfold before the riddle of the treasure is finally, excitingly solved?

FROM *LONDON* FAR

A random scrap of Augustan poetry muttered in a tobacconist's shop thrusts an absentminded scholar through a trapdoor into short-lived leadership of London's biggest art racket.

HAMLET, REVENGE!

The Lord Chancellor is shot in the midst of a private performance of *Hamlet*. Behind the scenes there are thirty-one suspects; in the audience, twenty-seven.

WHAT HAPPENED AT HAZELWOOD

Spend a weekend in the English countryside—old quarrels revived, unbridled sex . . . and murder all over the place!

Erskine Childers

THE RIDDLE OF THE SANDS

The Riddle of the Sands is regarded by many critics as one of the best spy novels ever written; it was certainly the first modern espionage story and remains a classic of the genre. Its unique flavor comes from its richly detailed technical background of inshore sailing in the Baltic and North seas, from its remarkable air of authenticity, and from its evocation of the world of the late 1890s, with its atmosphere of intrigue and mutual suspicion that was soon to lead to war. Erskine Childers died before a firing squad in Dublin, denounced as a traitor, yet his book was an expression of his loyalty to England and concern for the nation's defense. With its suspense-packed plot and breathtaking climax, it is a novel that will appeal to scores of readers brought up on the realism of Eric Ambler, Graham Greene, and John le Carré.

Jack London

THE ASSASSINATION BUREAU, LTD.

The Assassination Bureau kills people for money. It also has a social conscience. Determined to eliminate only society's enemies, its chief, Ivan Dragomiloff, decides whether or not each murder is "justified." One day Dragomiloff accepts a contract without knowing the name of the victim— and the person marked for death turns out to be himself. . . . Unfinished when Jack London died, this thrilling novel has been so successfully completed by Robert L. Fish that the reader is challenged to find the point where one writer stops and the other begins.

Sir Arthur Conan Doyle

THE MEMOIRS OF SHERLOCK HOLMES

Sir Arthur Conan Doyle was born in Edinburgh, Scotland, in 1859 and died in 1930. He studied medicine at Edinburgh University, where the diagnostic methods of one of the professors are said to have provided the idea for the methods of detection used by Sherlock Holmes. Doyle first set up as a doctor at Southsea, and it was while waiting for patients that he first began to write. His greatest achievement, of course, was his creation of Sherlock Holmes, who constantly diverted his creator from the work he preferred. *The Memoirs* consists of eleven adventures from the crowded life of Sherlock Holmes, including "The Final Solution," with which Doyle intended to close the career of his famous detective. Holmes was a match for the author, however, and the reading public's urgent pleas for further Holmes cases could not be resisted. Doyle was later compelled to resurrect him.

Edited by Hugh Greene

THE RIVALS OF SHERLOCK HOLMES

In these thirteen stories Hugh Greene gives enchanting proof that Sherlock Holmes stood by no means alone as a private detective in late-Victorian and Edwardian London. There were other narrow-eyed sleuths who assumed disguises, ordered private trains, and showered sovereigns on hansom-drivers. Some investigators, like Martin Hewitt and Dr. Thorndyke, are razor-sharp and sea-green incorruptible. Others, such as Romney Pringle and the sinister Dorrington, are equally acute but all out for themselves . . . and the devil take the law. Among the undeservedly forgotten authors are Max Pemberton, Arthur Morrison, Guy Boothby, William Le Queux, R. Austin Freeman, and Ernest Bramah—each successfully challenging Arthur Conan Doyle at his own game.

Three by Lionel Davidson

THE NIGHT OF WENCESLAS

Young Nicholas Whistler is trapped. "Invited" to Prague on what seems to be an innocent business trip, he finds himself caught between the secret police and the amorous clutches of the statuesque Vlasta. This first book established Lionel Davidson as a brilliant new novelist of action and adventure.

MAKING GOOD AGAIN

In Germany to settle a claim for reparation, lawyer James Raison is plunged into the old conflict between Jew and Nazi. His trip becomes more dangerous as the legal aspects of the case become more complicated, and at the same time he has to cope with his affair with Elke and his involvement with her fascist aunt, Magda. *Making Good Again* is the story not only of a complicated and exciting search for the true identity of the claimant but also of a search going on in the minds of the English, German, and Jewish lawyers—a search to discover and understand Nazi philosophy.

THE ROSE OF TIBET

Charles Houston had slipped illegally into Tibet to find his missing brother—only to be imprisoned in the forbidden Yamdring monastery. Now he has to get out of Tibet quickly, for the invading Chinese army and the cruel Himalayan winter are right behind him. . . . Daphne du Maurier wrote: "Is Lionel Davidson today's Rider Haggard? His novel has all the excitement of *She* and *King Solomon's Mines*."

Georges Simenon

MAIGRET AND THE ENIGMATIC LETT

Pietr the Lett has the personality of a chameleon. When crossing frontiers, he assumes all sorts of different identities—in addition to his amazing resemblance to the twisted corpse found in the toilet of the Pole Star Express. This is a bizarre case for Maigret!

MAIGRET AND THE HUNDRED GIBBETS

In a spirit of idle curiosity Maigret switches suitcases with a man at the German frontier, but when the traveler discovers the change, he takes out a gun and shoots himself. . . .

MAIGRET AT THE CROSSROADS

Twenty miles south of Paris they found the corpse of a Jewish diamond-merchant from Antwerp. Nobody knew a thing. Then the diamond-merchant's widow is shot down at Maigret's feet—and the chief inspector plunges into action.

MAIGRET GOES HOME

Was the countess murdered in the village church . . . or did she just give up breathing for Lent? Maigret uncovers six suspects—but none of them can ever be punished!

MAIGRET MYSTIFIED

Maigret uncovers a genteel underworld of old jealousies and stifled hatreds when he investigates the murder of M. Couchet, shot dead in the office of his pharmaceutical firm.

Also:

MAIGRET MEETS A MILORD
MAIGRET STONEWALLED
THE SAILORS' RENDEZVOUS

Graham Greene

THE POWER AND THE GLORY

In one of the southern states of Mexico, during an anticlerical purge, the last priest, like a hunted hare, is on the run. Too human for heroism, too humble for martyrdom, the little worldly "whiskey priest" is nevertheless impelled toward his squalid Calvary as much by his own efforts as by the efforts of his pursuers.

THE QUIET AMERICAN

The Quiet American is a terrifying portrait of innocence at large; it is also a wry comment on European interference in Asia in its story of the French-Vietminh war in Vietnam. While the French Army is grappling with the Vietminh, in Saigon a high-minded young American begins to channel economic aid to a "Third Force." The narrator, a seasoned foreign correspondent, is forced to observe, "I never knew a man who had better motives for all the trouble he caused."

SHADES OF GREENE

Eighteen of Graham Greene's finest short stories, which have been dramatized for television, devastatingly demonstrate his unique talent for exploring the subtleties of human relationships. Witty, sensitive, nightmarish, comic, or merciless, every story finds its echoes in the reader's own experience.

Also:

BRIGHTON ROCK
A BURNT-OUT CASE
THE COMEDIANS
THE END OF THE AFFAIR
THE HEART OF THE MATTER
IT'S A BATTLEFIELD
JOURNEY WITHOUT MAPS
LOSER TAKES ALL
MAY WE BORROW YOUR HUSBAND?
THE MINISTRY OF FEAR
THE PORTABLE GRAHAM GREENE
TRAVELS WITH MY AUNT